"Shall we cast a wager?"

Eleanore turned. "I beg your pardon?"

"A wager. On who will kiss whom first."

"You're mad."

"Is that a yes?"

Lukas could hear the words coming out of his mouth but he couldn't quite believe them. She'd aggravated him with the way she so easily froze him out. And the more she tried to mind her p's and q's with him the more he wanted to run roughshod all over them.

"How about if I kiss you first, you can have Harrington's name above the door of the hotel?"

Eleanore stilled. "Are you serious?"

"Why not?"

She couldn't believe he would wager that. "And what happens if I kiss you first?"

"Worried about your self-control, *moya krasavitsa*?"

She hated not knowing what he was calling her but she wouldn't lower herself to ask. Let him have his fun. Men and their egos.

The world's most elite hotel is looking for a jewel in its crown, and Spencer Chatsfield has found it. But Isabella Harrington, the girl from his past, refuses to sell!

Now the world's most decadent destinations have become a chessboard in this game of power, passion and pleasure...

Welcome to

The Chatsfield

Synonymous with style, sensation...and scandal!

With the eight Chatsfield siblings happily married and settling down, it's time for a new generation of Chatsfields to shine!

Spencer Chatsfield steps in as CEO, determined to prove his worth. But when he approaches Isabella Harrington, of Harringtons boutique hotels, with the offer of a merger that would benefit them both, he's left with a stinging red palm-shaped mark on his cheek!

And so begins a game of cat and mouse that will shape the future of the Chatsfields and the Harringtons forever.

But neither knows that there's one stakeholder with the power to decide their fate...and their identity will shock both the Harringtons *and* the Chatsfields.

Just who will come out on top?

Find out in:

Maisey Yates—**Sheikh's Desert Duty**

Abby Green—**Delucca's Marriage Contract**

Carol Marinelli—**Princess's Secret Baby**

Kate Hewitt—**Virgin's Sweet Rebellion**

Caitlin Crews—**Greek's Last Redemption**

Michelle Conder—**Russian's Ruthless Demand**

Susanna Carr—**Tycoon's Delicious Debt**

Melanie Milburne—**Chatsfield's Ultimate Acquisition**

Eight titles to collect—you won't want to miss out!

Michelle Conder

Russian's Ruthless Demand

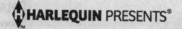

ISBN-13: 978-0-373-13820-3

Russian's Ruthless Demand

First North American publication 2015

Copyright © 2015 by Harlequin Books S.A.

Special thanks and acknowledgment are given to Michelle Conder for her contribution to The Chatsfield series.

Recycling programs for this product may not exist in your area.

www.Harlequin.com

Printed in U.S.A.

With two university degrees and a variety of false career starts under her belt, **Michelle Conder** decided to satisfy her lifelong desire to write and finally found her dream job. She currently lives in Melbourne, Australia, with one superindulgent husband, three self-indulgent (but exquisite) children, a menagerie of overindulged pets and the intention of doing some form of exercise daily. She loves to hear from her readers at michelleconder.com.

Books by Michelle Conder

Harlequin Presents

Dark, Demanding and Delicious

Scandal in the Spotlight

Visit the Author Profile page at Harlequin.com for more titles.

To Paul and our kids. Life got in the way a bit with this one but we made it through!

And to my fabulous editor, Laura McCallen. This book would not be here if not for your infinite patience and wonderful guidance. Thank you.

CHAPTER ONE

'YOU'RE BREAKING UP, PETRA. Who did you say quit?' Lukas Kuznetskov pressed his mobile phone closer to his ear, straining to hear as his PA explained the latest issue to befall the supposedly creative genius who had been hired to build his ice hotel. Apparently the man had stormed out after Lukas had questioned his latest set of drawings, complaining that Lukas was too controlling and stifled his creativity.

Creativity?

Lukas swore under his breath.

So far he had come up with the overall concept of the hotel himself while the architectural wizard he'd hired had done little more than fill in the technical details and organise the preliminary build. With only a month left until the most anticipated project in Russia was due to open it was fair to say Lukas was a little agitated. 'Please tell me he at least redesigned the interior of the guest bedrooms like I asked,' he growled, grinding his teeth when Petra confirmed that no, he had not.

Useless, lazy, good for nothing... Lukas sucked in a sharp breath as he strove for calm and told Petra he'd handle it. As if he wasn't busy enough.

'Trouble?'

Having momentarily forgotten his Italian ship engineer was in the room Lukas turned away from the splendour of Italy's Adriatic coastline and glanced at the plans laid out on a scored wooden table. They had just finished going over Tomaso's design for a supertanker that could carry twice as much cargo as any other on the market and go at twice the speed. If they could pull it off it would be another feather in Lukas's already well-plumed cap.

Tomaso Coraletti was as close to a friend as Lukas had ever allowed himself to have and the older man stroked his neat beard as Lukas updated him on his pet project.

'Biscotti, Lukas?'

Turning, Lukas replaced his scowl with a smile when he saw Tomaso's sweet wife, Maria, standing before him with a silver tray of freshly made biscotti in her hands. Tomaso reached across and took a piece before Lukas could respond and got his hand swatted for his efforts. 'Bah!' she scolded. 'Lukas is a growing boy. He needs it more than you.'

Tomaso scoffed and Lukas chuckled. He'd stopped growing a long time ago and they both knew it. '*Grazie mille*, Maria.' He took a slice of the treat even though he didn't want it and pocketed his phone.

'It is the best biscotti in the whole of Italy,' Tomaso boasted. 'Maybe one day you will be lucky enough to enjoy biscotti like this. If you're good.'

Lukas chuckled at Tomaso's pointed comment. He'd known Tomaso ever since he'd joined his first container ship as a deck boy. In fact, it had been Tomaso who had gotten him the job. He had been the ship's engineer and had convinced his brother, the captain, to give Lukas a trial. Lukas had been sixteen years old and living off the putrid streets of St Petersburg at the time but unlike the other street kids—his fellow troublemakers—he'd had ambition. Something the older man had recognised when Lukas intervened while a group of young thugs tried to fleece Tomaso of his pocket change. And maybe even his life.

Of course, Lukas hadn't trusted Tomaso's goodwill straightaway. While most of his peers sought safety in numbers, joining or forming gangs to keep them safe, Lukas kept to himself, learning at a young age that needing others was a one-way street to misery.

His loner days had started at the age of five when his mother had put him on a train from St Petersburg to Moscow and told him she'd meet him there. At the time he'd been terrified and young enough to believe she'd meant it. It had taken him another five years to make his way back to St Petersburg in his search for her. A wasted trip if ever there was one.

Realising he'd entered an almost trance-like state he gave himself a mental shake. Why dwell on all that now? So his architect had quit. It wasn't the worst that could happen and he'd succeed in the end. He always did. Like a phoenix rising from the ashes.

'No doubt you are indeed a lucky man, Tomaso,' he concurred, patting the old man on the shoulder. But really, Lukas knew that *he* was the lucky one. He was footloose and fancy-free and if he wanted biscotti he could go down to Harrods when he was in London or Gostiny Dvor in St Petersburg any time he wanted and buy an enormous amount. Not that it would be warm. And maybe not as flavoursome, but he was sure, if he ever wanted it, it would be decent. Biscotti was biscotti no matter how many ways you sliced it.

Maria pushed another three slices into his

hand, told him he worked too hard and needed to make babies instead of ships and left. He could have laughed. His last mistress had muttered the same complaint as she'd accepted the diamond necklace and Porsche Carrera on their final night together.

'I might know someone.'

Tomaso's statement brought Lukas's mind back to the job at hand. 'To make biscotti?'

'No.' He gave him a look. 'I leave the baby-making comments to *mia moglie*. I mean to help with your ice hotel.'

Lukas set the biscotti aside. 'At this point I'd hire a cartoon character if I thought he could do the job.'

Tomaso laughed. 'She's not a cartoon character, I can assure you, but she is good.'

'Who is she?'

'An ex-student of mine from Cornell and the daughter of the late boutique hotel owner, Jonathan Harrington.'

Lukas knew of the wealthy hotelier. He'd stayed in one of his hotels once and been less than impressed. He didn't know anything of his family except that they had no doubt lived a pampered existence. 'I know of the name.'

Hearing the shadow of scepticism in his voice, his friend said, 'Eleanore is the youngest of three daughters and extremely talented.'

He stroked his beard again. 'And from what I can tell, drastically underutilised in her current role at Harrington's.'

'She works for her family?' Lukas had never respected nepotism.

'Yes and I doubt it's nepotism if that's what you're thinking. Since her father passed away her sister Isabelle has run the show and she's one tough cookie.'

Lukas still wasn't convinced.

'If you don't believe me Eleanore just completed an ice bar in Singapore. It opens tomorrow as it turns out. I have an invitation but since her operation Maria doesn't like to travel.'

Lukas's ears pricked up. If the woman had designed an ice bar, then she understood the concept behind such an endeavour, and as he had the build in hand and only needed someone to fine-tune the design and do the internal fit-out she might just be what he was looking for.

And he respected Tomaso more than he did a lot of people which was why, the next day and despite some reservations as to her suitability, he was making a detour to Singapore on his way back to St Petersburg.

He glanced at the employee profile he'd pulled up on Eleanore Harrington en route.

She was marginally pretty with her creamy complexion and brownish coloured eyes, her wide smile that had probably financed some dentist's second holiday house. And there was something infinitely refined about her features that spoke more to hosting dinner parties in large houses than designing them. *Then getting naked in some man's bed. His bed.*

Lukas's brows drew down at the rogue thought. *Where had that come from?*

There was nothing special about Eleanore Harrington and he never mixed business with pleasure. Why complicate his place of solace with a woman bemoaning his perceived weaknesses as a man. 'You're too cold...' 'You're completely heartless...' 'You care about nobody but yourself...' All true and nothing he hid from any woman who occupied his bed. The trouble was *they* hid who they were from *him*. Right up until the end when they accepted his gifts and looked for another rich man to milk. Frankly the whole experience had started to pall.

He read further down Eleanore Harrington's profile. Graduating university with a major in architecture and a minor in interior design she had worked in her family's company from the get-go. Personal interests were reading, art, history, collecting shoes and volunteering at her local animal shelter.

Fascinating, Lukas thought dryly, thankful that he wasn't interested in her personally. She'd bore him to tears within minutes.

'We've started our descent into Singapore, Mr Kuznetskov. Can I get you anything else before we land, sir?'

'Nyet.' He stared out the window as the bright lights of Singapore came into view and hoped he wasn't wasting his time. He had a personal interest in making this venture a success so if Eleanore Harrington was half as good as Tomaso claimed she was he'd pretty much give her anything she wanted to get her on board.

Eleanore glanced at her watch for the hundredth time that night before swivelling around on her bar stool to stare at the main door. It opened and for a minute her heart lifted but it was only a merry group of Singapore's young urbanites who looked like they'd sipped one too many of Lulu's Yummy Yetis.

'You waiting for a lover?'

Eleanore pulled a face at Lulu's hopeful question and turned back to the bar, her eyes automatically drawn to Lulu's newly streaked purple hair that stood out even more beneath the colourful strobe lighting in the ice bar.

Lulu was the best bartender in New York City. She had also become a friend over the years she'd worked at Harrington's and Eleanore had brought her over especially for the opening night of their newest bar where everything—the bar top, the chairs, the stools, the walls and even the glasses—was made completely of compacted ice and snow. Quite the marvel in sultry Singapore and a roaring success according to the media heads who had come along for the free drinks and cocktails earlier on.

'My sisters,' she informed Lulu glumly.

Both Olivia and Isabelle had promised to attend the opening night of Glaciers to share in Eleanore's success but it was fairly safe to say that at close on midnight neither one was intending to show up. Not that Eleanore minded so much about Olivia not showing. She knew Olivia was busy with a new play about to open but Isabelle... Isabelle had the power to promote her to Harrington's executive team or not and being an integral part of her family's company was the most important thing in the world to Eleanore. It was what she strove for. It was what she got out of bed for in the mornings. And she'd been hoping that once Isabelle saw the incredible job she had done in designing the ice bar she would see that she was wasting her time redesigning cushion covers in hotel foyers or organising the latest colour schemes in the guest bedrooms, and offer her more.

Lulu put a frothy red concoction with a tiny umbrella sticking out the top in front of her and gave her a look that said she was a bitter disappointment to her friend. 'I knew a lover was too good to be true. Maybe you need to write it on your list of goals to make it happen.'

Eleanore pulled a face at Lulu's dig at her need to map her life out. It was her way of keeping her world in order and meeting a man was way down on the list at this stage of her life. 'I told you once before, career and men don't mix. Either they become snooty at how many hours I put in at work or they're so boring they make me want to stay at work for longer.' She glanced at the drink. 'What's this you've whipped up for me? After the last one I hope it has a low alcoholic content.' Especially since she couldn't remember if her last meal had been lunch or breakfast or dinner the night before.

She'd been running on adrenaline all day and guzzled coffee to keep herself going. Which was probably why she felt both buzzed and completely exhausted at the same time.

Lulu leaned one svelte hip against the bar, enjoying the lull in what had been a madcap

night. 'I'm calling it "Don't Poke the Bear."
Let me know what you think.' She gave the icy
bar another vigorous wipe. 'But don't get me
wrong. I'm not saying you should settle down.'
She gave a shiver as if the mere thought were
horrifying and pulled her ski gloves back on.
'But fun? Sex? When was the last time you
went out on a date?'

'Nineteen sixty-five,' Eleanore deadpanned.

Lulu laughed and pointed her cleaning rag at
her. 'I'd believe that. And it's exactly my point.
You need to get out more. Live a little.' Having
delivered her standard lecture she started lining up more shot glasses on the bar. 'So where
are your esteemed sisters anyway?'

It wasn't in Eleanore's nature to be pessimis-
tic but to assume they were stuck in traffic or
sitting on the tarmac at the airport was even
a stretch for her. 'Busy.' She heaved a sigh.
'Olivia is no doubt auditioning for some play
somewhere and this whole drama of the Chatsfields trying to take us over seems to have consumed every one of Isabelle's waking hours.'
And even now Eleanore could picture Isabelle
holed up with the horrible Spencer Chatsfield
in some argument.

Probably Eleanore needed to be a little more
understanding. Only it was hard to indulge her
understanding side when she had been to al-

most every one of Olivia's opening nights and every important event in Isabelle's calendar.

'Well, that's good,' Lulu said briskly. 'It gives you time to play. And sex will definitely make you feel better.'

Eleanore raised a brow and caught sight of her disgruntled expression in the mirrored wall behind the bar. She thought about texting Isabelle and then changed her mind. What was she going to say? That she was disappointed with her no-show? Her sister would likely frown and ask why. It wouldn't occur to her that Eleanore had always felt like she was on the outside looking in. It wouldn't occur to Isabelle that Eleanore questioned her place in the family because Isabelle was always so smart and successful and Olivia so beautiful and talented. And as for sex making her feel better... She rolled her eyes at Lulu's suggestion. 'So will a hot bath,' she said. 'And a tub of Ben & Jerry's Cookies and Cream.'

Lulu waggled a dark eyebrow. 'But can a hot bath give you a screaming orgasm and then make you a cup of hot cocoa afterward?'

Eleanore sipped her cocktail. 'If you've found a man who will make you a cup of *any-thing* after sex I suggest you keep him. Most of the stories I've heard are from women who are screaming at their man who rolls over straight after sex and goes to sleep—orgasm not guaranteed.' Not that she had any personal experience with that. The timing, the opportunity and the desire to have sex just hadn't come together for her yet.

'Speaking of orgasms…' Lulu's voice lowered by about ten octaves. 'Have a look at what the cat just dragged in.' She leant her elbows on the bar. 'A sexy, lonely businessman looking for some company for the night.'

'He's probably married.' Eleanore glanced up at the mirror and caught a glimpse of cropped dirty-blond hair, a Viking-hard face and powerful shoulders encased in a heavy black cloak. His tall frame oozed power and authority and he scanned the room as if he were the next line of terminators come back from the past to decimate someone. He was also without a doubt the most striking man Eleanore had ever seen and then his blue eyes connected with hers and her stinky mood hit a new low.

She knew him.

'I think the ice bar is starting to melt,' Lulu murmured, fanning her face with one of her ski gloves.

'Don't waste your breath,' Eleanore advised. 'He's a complete jackass.'

'You know him?' Lulu's tone was awestruck.

'I know *of* him.' Lukas Kuznetskov—billionaire businessman who guarded his privacy like a lion guards its pride and who was revered for being both enigmatic and ruthless. She'd only ever seen him in person one time at a fashion event she'd been lucky enough to score an invite to a year ago. He'd been dating the lead model at the time and he had reminded Eleanore of a peacock strutting around with her afterward. It had been a competition as to who had been the most beautiful. 'He's one of those superficial guys who are too good-looking and too wealthy for their own good.'

'I'm not against superficial as long as it's good in bed and something tells me that he is.'

Eleanore glanced up and found him watching her. A strange sensation zinged through her body and her breathing was a little quick as she forced her attention back to Lulu. 'Believe me, he's so self-important he'd be too concerned with his own pleasure to worry about yours and you could forget that hot chocolate afterward. You'd be lucky to see the door close as he ran through it.'

Lulu eyed her suspiciously. 'You have a very strong opinion of him…' She let her voice taper off and Eleanore knew what she was thinking. That she liked him. Nothing could be further from the truth. Two years ago, just before her father had passed away, he'd made a horribly disparaging comment about one of their hotels that had affected their brand for months afterward.

'It's not what you think,' she said emphatically. 'I can't stand the man.'

'Well, he's definitely interested in you because he keeps looking this way.' Lulu leaned across the bar. 'I dare you to flirt with him.'

'Oh, please,' Eleanore scoffed. 'He's so obnoxious and self-important I'd rather flirt with a snake.'

'I hope you don't mean me, Miss Harrington.'

Eleanore's stomach dropped into her numb toes as she realised that Lulu's position in front of her had blocked his approach in the mirrored wall and that she'd been clearing her throat for a reason.

She glanced sideways and up and her heart stuttered inside her chest at his amused half smile. He didn't believe she'd been talking about him at all. He was just trying to be charming.

Wishing he didn't know who she was she put on her professional face and decided to skip over his question. 'Good evening. Welcome to Glaciers.'

It was an automatic greeting rather than a sincere one but he didn't seem smart enough to pick that up.

'Thank you,' he murmured in a voice designed for radio—or the bedroom. 'You created this ice bar, I understand.'

It wasn't so much a question as a statement and Eleanore forced herself to focus on who he was and not how he looked or sounded. 'Yes.'

'It's spectacular. Congratulations.'

The way his gaze held hers made Eleanore's breath quicken. He was the spectacular one. His eyes so blue it was like looking at a cloudless summer sky. Her eyes drifted over his face. Straight nose, high cheekbones and a carved jaw not even the hint of a beard growth could soften.

No, he wasn't spectacular, she amended silently. Spectacular was somehow too girlie for a man who reeked of power and authority. Someone so confidently male. Or maybe he just seemed that way because of the scar that cut through the edge of his left eyebrow as if someone had taken to him with a knife.

'Cat got your tongue?'

Maybe an ex-girlfriend, she thought churlishly as she realised she had been caught staring. She chugged down the last of Lulu's lethal cocktail and composed herself. 'Not at all,' she said smoothly. 'I was just thinking about leaving.'

'But I have only just arrived.'

Was she supposed to care about that?

'Can I get you a drink, sir?' Lulu asked in her most deferential bartender voice, and Eleanore wondered absently if he had ever come across a woman who didn't want him. Probably not with his looks and money, and she decided that she quite enjoyed the thought of being the first.

'A Stoli if you have it. Neat.'

'Coming right up,' Lulu chirped.

Eleanore nearly rolled her eyes. She wanted to tell Lulu to dial it down a little but settled for thinking of a polite way to extricate herself from his presence instead.

'Would you like a refill?'

It took a moment for her to realise he was talking to her and Eleanore shook her head and felt slightly dizzy. Damned that 'Don't Poke the Bear' drink. 'No, thanks.'

About to slide her now completely numb bottom off the sheepskin-covered ice stool she sensed him move beside her and glanced up.

The look he settled on her made that strange sensation return and his thick brows drew together when she shivered.

'You are cold. You should be wearing a

jacket in here. It must be minus six at least.' His voice was a low murmur and before Eleanore could protest he'd whisked his heavy black cloak from his wide shoulders and dwarfed her in its warmth.

For a moment she couldn't move. The heady scent of clean, spicy male saturated her senses and robbed her of breath. Which made her feel downright foolish because she wasn't the kind of woman to be taken in by a smooth talker like this. It had to be Lulu's comments about flirting and sex making her feel so unlike herself. And the silly cocktails she'd consumed, of course.

Mr Smooth-Talking Kuznetskov leant his elbow against the bar and drew her attention to the thin cotton shirt that moulded itself to his impressive chest and tapered down to a lean waist before tucking into custom-tailored black pants. He wore highly polished dress shoes she knew hadn't come from any High Street trader, elevating his aura of brute male elegance.

He shifted under the weight of her sizzling gaze and when Eleanore raised her eyes to his she was glad of the strobe lighting that hopefully hid the blush that crept into her cheeks. Pop music blared from the speaker system and she focused in on it as if she'd been absorbed by that and not his masculinity for the past couple of minutes.

A small smile played around the edges of his mouth as if she hadn't fooled him one bit and it was all the impetus she needed to pull the cloak from her shoulders and push off the ice stool to stand beside him. With his slouched position and her high-heeled boots they were at eye level and Eleanore thrust the cloak out in front of her. 'I don't need this.' No, she needed a hit around the head for being such a dunce!

His eyes narrowed, his gaze assessing. 'That dress can't be keeping you very warm.'

Eleanore arched a brow, determined not to fall prey to his deadly good looks. He was right, of course; her thin woollen dress was completely inappropriate for the low temperature inside the bar but she'd been running on adrenaline all night and hadn't noticed. And she had a jacket. She just couldn't remember where she had put it. 'Whether it is or not is hardly any business of yours.'

His own brow arched. 'Indeed.'

'Yes.' The smile she gave him was brittle at best because she wanted him to know that he was wasting his time trying to pick her up—if that was his intention—and why else would he bother with the compliments and inane chit-chat if it wasn't? 'I hope you enjoy the ice bar.

We'd love to see you here again sometime but…'

She frowned when he threw his head back and laughed. 'You find something amusing?'

'Only that you're frostier than the bar top I'm leaning on.' He raised his arm and they both glanced at the wet circle around his elbow. Eleanore was about to say something pithy about not leaning on frozen water when she realised how tall and broad he was compared to her own five feet four—or seven in her ankle boots.

'And somehow I seem to have offended you without even trying,' he continued charmingly. 'But perhaps that is because I have forgotten to introduce myself. I am Lukas Kuznetskov.'

'I know who you are.' The words were out before Eleanore could recall them and they sank between them like rocks thrown into a murky pond.

Lukas remained completely still as he registered the insult implicit in her tone. Perhaps that comment he'd overheard earlier between her and Miss Gothic had been about him after all.

Eleanore's eyes flashed tiny green and amber sparks at him and he realised absently that they were hazel, not brown as he'd first thought. Alluring eyes that tilted a little at the edges in line with her cheekbones.

When he'd first arrived he'd thought she looked quite dowdy sitting on the stool in a basic black dress, the only colour coming from a pair of bright orange ankle boots that tended to make a woman's ankles look twice the size they were and some weird matching chopstick things sticking out of her neat bun. Then her interesting eyes had caught his in the mirror and briefly stalled his train of thought. Once he'd shaken off the weird feeling that a goose had just walked over his grave he'd studied her. He'd waited for her covetous gaze to signal the type of interest he was used to getting from women. But she hadn't done that. Instead she'd grimaced as if she'd just been shown a bag full of eels and looked away.

His healthy ego had felt the immediate prick of her dismissal but he'd thought she didn't know who he was. He'd assumed that when she found out she'd be more than happy to talk to him. And probably warm his bed if he was so inclined. Which he wasn't. Under different circumstances he might have been drawn to her elegant features and full lips. Those cat-like eyes, but he had a different agenda tonight and it didn't include taking her to his bed.

Still, he couldn't fathom her negative re-

sponse other than to think that she was one of
those phony stuck-up rich girls who thought
pedigree was everything. He'd learned the hard
way that just because he now knew his fish
fork from his fruit fork it didn't mean instant
acceptance from those with old money.

Fortunately he was sufficiently impressed
with the overall effect and intricate detail put
into Glaciers, not to mention being up against
the clock, to set aside his own misgivings about
her suitability for his project to offer her a job.
First though he'd have to find a way to thaw
her out. A not altogether displeasing concept.

'Why do I get the feeling you dislike me,
Miss Harrington?'

'I don't dislike you at all, Mr Kuznetskov.'
She gave him another false smile and squared
her slender shoulders. 'How could I when I
don't even know you? And I'm certainly not
the type of person to make a snap judgement
on such a brief acquaintance,' she finished
primly.

Da, *she disliked him all right.* 'I think you're
lying, Miss Harrington,' he said pleasantly.

The bartender pushed an ice glass across
to him, interrupting Eleanore Harrington's
shocked gasp, and he downed the finger of
vodka in one hit and welcomed the burn of it
down the back of his throat.

'I am not.'

'Yes, you are. For some reason you've not only judged me, you've sentenced me as well, and yet by your own admission we don't even know each other.'

'Would that be like you passing judgement on our hotels two years ago when you had only stayed one night?' she challenged.

Ah, Lukas was beginning to understand her animosity now. Somehow she'd heard about his comments after his brief stay at her Florida hotel. Not that he would apologise for them. He'd suffered a terrible night's sleep on a lumpy mattress and then his morning coffee had been cold. On top of that the valet had misplaced his car and he'd been overcharged on his bill. All in all, not a great experience. 'My comments were deserved, Miss Harrington. Your hotel offered substandard service and I said as much.'

'To the press?' She crinkled her pretty nose. 'I could have respected your comments if you'd filled out a hospitality card but instead you had to announce your views to the world. You do know that our occupancy rate went down twenty percent for six months after that.'

Lukas could feel himself getting annoyed with her attitude. 'I don't believe I have quite that much influence in the world—though, of course, I'm flattered that you do. Perhaps your lower occupancy rate was due to management issues.'

'Oh, you would take that view.'

'If it helps, I didn't mean for my comments to make it to the press,' he offered. 'In fact, I didn't even know that they had.'

'How could you not?' She reluctantly perched on the edge of her stool when she realised they were drawing curious glances from nearby patrons.

'I don't read my own press. I pay someone to do that and to bring anything that needs addressing to my attention. Clearly that was not big enough to warrant my attention.'

'Clearly not.' Her pointy little chin rose between them. 'Goodnight, Mr Kuznetskov.'

'Hold on.' Lukas put his gloved hand out and snagged her delicate wrist just above where her own dark gloves ended. 'So, based on my truthful comments you've made an assumption that I'm a bad person, is that it?'

Well, it had been that and the way he had swanned through the world as if he owned it, Eleanore thought acidly. The way she had wished that she had been the one on his arm at the fashion show instead of that stunning model. 'I'm entitled to my opinion,' she said, and nearly winced at how much she sounded like a schoolmarm from a bad nineteen-fifties sitcom.

'Yes, you are. And fortunately for you I'm sufficiently impressed with your ice bar to continue this conversation.'

What did that mean?

'Can I get that on record?' she asked archly.

He smiled. 'Like I said, it's nice to know you think my opinion is so powerful.'

Oh, he knew his opinion was powerful. He spoke and the press behaved like pathetic lapdogs. As did his women, no doubt. 'Why should how you feel about Glaciers make any difference to me?'

'Because I have an opportunity to offer you.'

An opportunity? Eleanore nearly laughed. Only he could call picking up a woman in a bar an *opportunity.* 'Not interested,' she said flatly.

He paused and shook his head. 'My, how you do like to jump to conclusions, Miss Harrington. But I didn't mean that kind of opportunity.' His gaze raked her over and sent hot rivulets of sensation sparking through her. 'Although I could be persuaded to consider the other if you were so inclined.'

Irritation, she thought sourly, that was what had caused the strange sensation to suffuse her body, that and the fact that she had somehow amused him without intending to. 'I'm not. And nor am I interested in any *opportunity* you might have for me, Mr Kuznetskov. Is that clear enough for you?' She smiled with false sweetness, extricating her wrist from his firm grip.

Lukas laughed again. He hadn't expected to enjoy himself quite so much when he'd arrived in Singapore. He hadn't expected to find the Harrington heiress so alluring either. 'You know it's very—how do you say?—gender specific to let your emotions make your decisions for you,' he drawled, admiring the way her eyes sparkled and her cheeks grew a little flushed as he challenged her.

'And it's very—how do you say?—gender specific for you to not take no for an answer,' she retorted.

His grin widened at her heated comeback. 'Touché, Miss Harrington.' He held out his hand. 'Shall we start over?'

'I don't see why we should.'

'Because as I said I have an opportunity— a possible *job* opportunity—to discuss with you.'

'A job? Are you joking?'

'I never joke about business.'

'Well, I already have a job.'

'One where you are currently underutilised.'

'How would you know that?'

Lukas nearly shook his head at her shocked outburst. Did the woman not know how to hide any of her emotions? 'Tomaso Coraletti.'

She tilted her head to the side. 'How do you know Tomaso?'

'He builds ships for me.'

'Well, that's a relief,' she scorned. 'For a moment I thought his taste in friends had plummeted.'

Lukas smiled. If she was trying to put him off by being contrary it wasn't working. In fact, the more riled she became, the more her interesting eyes sparkled and the more his body stirred. A realisation that surprised him. Perhaps Maria was right and he needed to go find himself some biscotti. Some very *temporary* biscotti. 'He said you were one of the most talented students he's ever taught and that you would be perfect for the project I am working on.'

'Well, that's very nice of him but it doesn't change the fact that you've wasted your time coming here because...'

'Look, Miss Harrington,' Lukas interrupted, short of patience and time and not a little put out by his unexpected physical reaction to her. 'You've voiced your unhappiness at my comments about your hotels and it's been duly noted but business is business. It would be a mistake to confuse it with anything personal.'

'Excuse me?' Her chin came up. 'Are you implying that I am?'

Clearly he'd hit a nerve.

She stood up quickly, nearly overbalancing her stool, and would have stumbled if he hadn't reached out and grabbed her elbow.

'What are you doing?' she grated at him. 'Let me go.'

He could feel the delicate bones of her arm through his gloves and slowly pulled his hand away. 'My apologies,' he drawled, somewhat disconcerted by the thought that he'd like to remove his glove and touch her bare skin with his own. 'Should I have let you fall?' he mocked. 'I'm never sure with you card-carrying feminists.'

'Very funny.'

Giving himself a mental shakedown Lukas got his mind back on track. 'Or perhaps you just don't think you can do it.'

Eleanore couldn't believe the gall of the man. First he insulted her business and then he insulted her. About to lambast the man, the enormous overhead fan kicked in and a blast of cold air shot out of the vents and cooled her heated cheeks. It also blew the loose strands of her hair across her face.

Pulling off a glove she reached up to carefully dislodge the hair that had snagged on her lipstick when her fingers collided with his. Apparently Lukas had also removed his glove and she knew a moment of absolute shock as the feel of his warm skin against hers zinged through her system in a flash of sexual heat. Like a cyborg waking from a deep sleep, parts of her body came online for the first time and her dazed eyes landed on his sculpted lips so close to her own.

'An ice hotel,' he murmured, his gaze lingering on her mouth as if he knew she had been wondering what it would be like to breach the insignificant gap between them and kiss him.

Flustered, annoyed and tired, Eleanore glared at the man. 'I beg your pardon?'

'I'm building an ice hotel and my architect just quit. I want you to complete the design and project-manage the build.'

An ice hotel? A whole ice hotel? For a moment all Eleanore's other senses came to full attention. She'd tried to convince Isabelle to do an ice hotel in Canada the year before but she had thought it a waste of time and money. 'Why did your architect quit?'

'Because his ego was larger than his talent.'

Eleanore's lips quirked at his incongruous

statement. 'I'm sure he didn't phrase it like that.'

'Perhaps not.' He gave her a slow smile. 'But I can see I have your attention now.'

Annoyed at the victorious gleam in his eyes she shook her head. 'Which part of *no* didn't you get, Mr Kuznetskov? The *n* or the *o*?'

'I don't tend to respond that well to the word *no*,' he drawled.

'Then you haven't wasted your time coming here after all because you're about to be taught an important life lesson. And anyway, my sister would never agree to it.'

Isabelle had been even angrier about Lukas's disparaging comments two years ago than Eleanore had been.

'Well, that's too bad.' He shrugged. 'Perhaps I'll approach Spencer Chatsfield and see what he can do for me.'

Spencer Chatsfield? He was probably the only other man Isabelle disliked more. And what did Lukas know about their current feud? 'Is that some sort of threat?' she asked incredulously.

'I never make threats.' His smoking-hot grin told her he knew he had her. 'I'm in room 1006 if you change your mind.'

'We don't have a room 1006.'

His grin faded into a cocky smile as if he

knew his next words would choke her. 'Room 1006 at The Chatsfield.'

And he was right.

Eleanore blinked as he strode unhurriedly from the bar, his loose-limbed grace drawing both male and female glances his way.

Arrogant, horrible...

'That got a little heated,' Lulu said, materialising at her side.

She wasn't kidding.

Eleanore frowned. 'Have you seen my phone?'

'Yeah.' She reached behind an ice shelf on the bar. 'I put it here when we got busy before and forgot to tell you.'

Picking it up Eleanore tried to get her cold fingers to work long enough to call Isabelle. It was still early in New York—if in fact her sister was even in New York—but she still couldn't get through to her.

About to leave a message, she hung up. Would Lukas Kuznetskov really approach the Chatsfields for help with his ice hotel? And if he did what would Isabelle say if she knew Eleanore had passed up the opportunity to get in first?

'I'm in room 1006 if you change your mind.'

Arrogant, horrible...

Annoyed Eleanore downed a glass of water

on the bar and only realised halfway through that it wasn't water.

Lulu smacked her on the back repeatedly as she went into a coughing fit. 'Honey, that was straight tequila,' she advised.

Eleanore dabbed at her watering eyes. 'It's in a water glass,' she wheezed.

'We ran out of shot glasses.'

Great. A burnt oesophagus on top of everything else. What more could go wrong tonight?

CHAPTER TWO

TEN MINUTES LATER Eleanore found herself in a cab outside the main entrance of The Chatsfield, Singapore.

She glanced out the window, scouting for any paparazzi lurking in the shadows. Fortunately no one was around other than a liveried doorman and she steeled her spine as he reached out to open her door.

Deciding that the best way to go unnoticed was to act like she was just another guest coming in late for the night, she smiled confidently at the doorman as she strode past.

Once through the gleaming glass doors she crossed the acre of white-and-blue-veined marble floors toward the wall of gleaming elevators, hoping that none of the Chatsfields were in residence. Running into one of them would be truly humiliating!

If it was possible, she hated Lukas Kuznetskov even more for putting her in this nerve-wracking situation and only exhaled when the lift doors closed behind her, sealing her into its mirrored vault.

One mission accomplished without incident, she thought with a relieved breath. Maybe the rest of the night would go the same way.

She took a moment to study her reflection, smoothing out the lipstick she'd taken the time to reapply before leaving her hotel, and checked that her hair was still in place. No way was she meeting Mr Smooth-Talking Kuznetskov on his turf looking like one of Lulu's wrung-out dish rags.

Satisfied, she raised her eyes to track the ascending numbers on the lift panel and wondered again if she shouldn't have left this meeting until morning. Then she decided that no, she was unlikely to fall asleep with Lukas's 'opportunity' hanging over her head and— some wicked side she never would have guessed she possessed—hoped she might interrupt *his* sleep as payment for his arrogance.

Unfortunately he wasn't sleeping, he was on the phone when he answered the door, and he didn't even pause in his conversation as he ushered her inside. She noticed that he'd rolled his shirtsleeves to his elbows and ignored the temptation to admire his impressive forearms. So the man had a good body. That didn't make him an attractive person. A man needed a lot more than money and looks to get her attention.

'Arrogant jackass,' she murmured under her breath as she stalked past him, stopping in the centre of the spacious sitting room, her designer's eye admiring the rich furnishings and sophisticated fittings.

Still talking on the phone he bent over the low coffee table between two large sofas and pressed a few keys on his laptop. Then he swivelled the computer toward her and indicated for her to take a seat. 'Have a look at these,' he murmured before returning his attention to his caller.

Rude was the only word that came to Eleanore's mind and she resented the superior way he thought he'd won. She had half a mind to ignore his computer but that left only him to look at so she relented. And anyway, she reminded herself, she was here to stop him from offering someone at the Chatsfield Hotels a job until she had a chance to consider his proposal properly. Not that she imagined for one minute that Isabelle would be happy with her being here. Which made her incredibly uncomfortable because she adored her sister and would never do anything to upset her.

A minute later a fresh bottle of water was

plonked down in front of her. She glanced up and a smile tilted the corner of his lips as if he knew exactly how disgruntled she was. Which was impossible. She wasn't *that* easy to read. Was she?

'Sorry about the phone call. Unfortunately business doesn't sleep.'

The mention of sleep made her think of beds and tiredness and him and she shook off a wooziness probably brought about by the tequila slammer she'd inadvertently ingested.

'Are you sure you don't want coffee? You look like you could use it.'

'Thanks,' she said tartly, knowing that even if she was dying for a cup she wouldn't take one from him after that. 'I'm perfectly fine.' Now if he'd offered her a chocolate brownie with vanilla ice cream on the side she might have set her pride aside. Okay, she *would* have, but coffee would only keep her up anyway.

He shrugged at her response and sat down on the sofa beside her. The cushion bowed under his extra weight and she felt herself list toward him and had to put her hand down between their bodies to stop herself from touching him. Even so, her hand brushed the hard muscle of his thigh and she shifted away as if she was politely giving him more space when in reality his closeness seemed to addle her thinking. Or was that the cocktail and tequila? Either way Eleanore wanted to get this out of the way and get back to her bed. Alone.

Well, of course alone, she admonished the voice in her head. She had little time or inclination for a man as it was and this man would never make her top one hundred, let alone her top ten. 'So tell me what I'm looking at,' she said briskly.

He clicked the mouse a couple of times and a three-dimensional snowflake came onto the screen. 'The hotel is designed to look like a snowflake. Five wings hold the guest bedrooms and one is the reception area and main restaurant.' He scrolled through a few more images and despite her determination to be bored by the whole thing she wasn't.

'It's very clever,' she conceded reluctantly.

'A compliment, Eleanore?'

'Don't take it to heart, Mr Kuznetskov.' She didn't like the way he said her name. It sounded too familiar on his lips. Too sexy coming from that deeply accented voice.

He smiled as if he could read her like an open book. 'It is clever, but I need someone to turn it from a concept into a reality. Can you do it?'

Could she do it? Yes, she had no doubt she could—or at least she hoped she could. Would she give him the upper hand by revealing that? Never.

'You might want to think about moving the restaurant so that it's more central to the design,' she said before she could stop herself.

His brows drew together. 'I already thought of that but I was told it wasn't possible due to the positioning of the kitchen.'

Eleanore stifled a yawn as her creative side warred with her need to get up and leave. 'It is. You just have to know how to do it.'

'And you know how.'

'Yes, actually, I do. I was fascinated by the concept of living in an igloo as a child and incorporated ice buildings as one of my electives during my final year of study.' She frowned at the screen. 'The guest bedrooms are also a little...'

'Dull?'

His straightforwardness was refreshing, she thought. Too often people tried to cover up inadequacies or mistakes with excuses. 'Yes, that word works. These rooms are basically designed all the same. If you want to be truly innovative you need to have them themed.'

'What do you mean?'

'I mean, give your guests a reason to visit other than for a night sleeping in a fridge. Which is essentially what they're getting.'

'This hotel will be pure luxury. Whatever guests want they'll have.'

'To make it pure luxury on ice you'll need designer rooms and a warm bathroom to be attached to each one.'

'I was told that couldn't be done either.'

She shook her head when she realised how far she had been drawn in by him. 'Why do I feel like I'm being manipulated?'

He smiled and it belonged to a movie star. 'What about the atrium in the reception area? I know there's something wrong with it but I can't pick it.'

Eleanore knew she shouldn't look. 'It needs to be larger. The way it is now the spacing is all wrong and the reception desk is too close to the entrance.'

'That's it.' He shot her an admiring glance. 'I do believe you might be the genius.'

About to tell him that compliments didn't work on her, his phone rang and he pulled it out of his pocket and glanced at the screen. 'Excuse me, I have to take this.'

Releasing a pent-up breath, Eleanore's eyes followed the long line of his body as he strode to the windows and looked out as he talked; legs planted wide apart, his gaze high as if he was a general surveying a battlefield he was about to conquer.

A wave of tiredness hit her like a brick wall and she yawned and rested her head back against the soft cushion behind her. She would tell him she was leaving as soon as he finished up on his call and talk to him after she'd spoken to Isabelle.

And she'd also find out the name of the company that supplied the hotel's soft furnishings because this was possibly *the* most comfortable sofa she had ever sat on.

When Lukas ended his phone call he turned back to find Eleanore Harrington had fallen asleep. He stood over her, watching the slow rise and fall of her chest as she breathed deeply. His eyes travelled lower to where her dress had risen to just above mid-thigh. She had fabulous legs. Shorter than he was used to because he didn't date petite women, but no less shapely. And she still had on her brightly coloured ankle boots that somehow didn't make her ankles look fat at all.

He almost felt like a voyeur watching her in her unconscious state. Or maybe it was that in sleep her face looked strangely innocent. Strangely…pure.

An odd sensation constricted his chest. *Pure?* He was surprised he even remembered the term, let alone recognised the quality. Pure and innocent hadn't been part of his life since conception probably and he wondered how he could attribute the term to a woman who had gone toe to toe with him earlier over the slight he had caused to her family's company.

He briefly considered waking her but she looked so peaceful he didn't have the heart.

Instead he let his eyes drift back over her slender torso to her breasts that were well hidden by her plain dress and up to the quirky chopsticks she had in her caramel-brown hair. They couldn't be comfortable and he had an impulsive urge to pull them out to see how long her hair was. To see it tumble down her back and spread out over the cream-coloured sofa.

Then he shook off the thought and frowned when he realised that his hands had moved closer to her to do exactly that. Diverting them to her feet he unzipped her boots and gently placed her feet up on the sofa. Immediately her body pitched more horizontal and her lovely legs curled up toward her chest in a child's pose.

Lukas felt his body stir again and clamped down on it. He couldn't deny that on some level she intrigued him and he'd certainly enjoyed himself tonight more than he'd enjoyed himself in a long time, but success was everything, and no slip of a woman would ever interfere with that.

He thought again about how she had taken him on over his criticism of her hotel. Probably she had been right to call him on it but the shock of having someone question his actions after being revered for so long had kept him from agreeing with her. Really though, she was right and he should have tabled his complaints appropriately instead of mouthing off on his phone to his PA.

Frowning, he wondered when he'd become such a self-important *popka*.

Not enjoying the unexpected attack of his conscience he fetched a blanket from the bedroom and draped it over her sleeping form. The chopsticks he left well enough alone.

When she woke up Eleanore blinked and wondered if someone had stuck her eyes together last night with glue. She lifted her hands to rub at them and felt the stiffness of her eyelashes and realised she'd gone to bed without taking her make-up off. Something she never did.

Still tired, she yawned and rolled over and felt the pull of her dress. Blinking herself awake she frowned as she realised she hadn't taken her dress off either. Or her stockings.

And she was on a sofa with a light blanket thrown over her. 'What the…?'

'Morning, *spyashchaya krasavitsa*.'

Startled, Eleanore's hand flew to her chest as her eyes flew to the man leaning nonchalantly against the doorjamb. He was dressed in suit pants again and another pristine white shirt, open at the neck. She'd seen many men wear similar outfits at work over and over without noticing the width of their shoulders or the narrowness of their hips but there was something in the way Lukas carried himself that drew the eye like a moth to a flame.

Suddenly the events of last night came back in a rush and she realised she'd dreamt about his ice hotel. And him…

He strolled further into the room and she noticed he had a tall glass of water in his hand and that her mouth was as dry as dust. She also had the makings of a dull headache but it wasn't enough to waylay her.

When he handed her the glass she drank from it greedily.

'Thanks.' She glanced around the room. Anywhere but at him. Then she frowned. 'You should have woken me last night.'

'I didn't need the sofa.'

Eleanore placed the empty glass on the table. 'That's no excuse.'

'I did take off your boots but you were so out of it I don't think you would have woken up if an earthquake had hit.'

She grimaced. 'It must have been the alcohol. I'm not used to it.'

'There is lots of alcohol in St Petersburg. You will have plenty of opportunities to build your stamina if you work for me.'

Eleanore narrowed her eyes. 'You're glad that I stayed, aren't you?'

'I wouldn't say glad but if you mean it gives me an advantage in getting what I want, then yes, I suppose you could say I'm glad.'

'And you want me?'

As the silence between them lengthened Eleanore realised what she'd said. 'I meant to work for you. Obviously.'

He smiled. '*Da*. Yes. To work for me.'

Eleanore shook her head. 'I would never leave my job. My heart is with Harrington's.'

'And do you always follow your heart?'

Did she? 'Yes, I suppose I do. My family means a lot to me. And they need me.' At least she hoped that was true.

'Staying in a company for family reasons can limit your true potential.'

Eleanore felt the pointy edge of that comment and it raised her hackles. 'That's cynical.'

Unperturbed by her put-down he shrugged.

'Tomaso seems to think you have enormous potential that is not being tapped where you currently are. I'm willing to back it. How do you take your coffee?'

'At my hotel,' Eleanore said churlishly, annoyed at his barbs and the way he chuckled at her response. He had a habit of laughing at her and it was getting under her skin. Still, she needed to keep him onside if she was to talk to Isabelle about his ice hotel. And preferably before he contacted the Chatsfields. She wouldn't work for him directly, but that didn't mean Harrington's couldn't do something for him. If Isabelle agreed… 'Which I need to get back to,' she said briskly. 'I'll contact you later with regard to your proposition.'

He shook his head. 'While I admire your loyalty to your family and I'm sure they appreciate it I need to move on this now if the hotel is going to be ready for opening night in a month.'

'A month!' Her eyebrows shot up. 'How much of it is already completed?'

He counted a list off with his fingers. 'The ice blocks have been harvested and stacked in the warehouse, the arched corridors are done and waiting to be tractored onto the site. The vaulted steel support walls are up, and the construction crew and some of the ice carvers are in place.'

'That's not a lot.' She did some calculations in her head. 'I'd say a month is leaning heavily on the optimistic side of things.'

'So you'll do it?'

'I didn't say that,' she said, feeling railroaded.

'Why don't you go and freshen up and think about it? I need your answer now. This morning.'

'That's impossible.'

He shrugged. 'I have found nothing is impossible, Miss Harrington, for good or bad.'

Something in his tone, a bleakness, hit her in the stomach and made her pause. Unable to understand it she frowned. 'I can't decide about this on the spot.'

He folded his arms across his impressive chest and she wondered how he managed to look so fresh on probably less sleep than she had had. 'Why? Do you not have the authority to make the decisions?'

No, she didn't. But that was another thing she wouldn't tell him. 'Businesses don't function like that.'

'I'm only asking for a month of your time. If you can't do it say so now.'

Fuming at him and desperate to use the bathroom she shoved the blanket aside—refusing to see it as a thoughtful gesture on his behalf—and swung her legs over the edge of the sofa. Her dress was bunched up around her hips and she flushed as she noticed Lukas's eyes drop to her legs.

Expecting him to make some sexist comment she was surprised when he turned away toward the window instead. Another nice gesture? Probably not.

Escaping to the bathroom she was appalled to see she looked like a bad rendition of a panda. A panda with really bad hair.

Well, was it any wonder he'd turned away? She was about as attractive as... She stopped. Stared at herself.

'You do not want that man to find you attractive no matter what you think,' she told her wide-eyed reflection.

So he was good-looking. Since when had she been shallow enough to want a man for his looks? His body?

Disgusted with her train of thought she splashed warm water onto her face and used a cloth to scrub the excess of make-up away and wished she hadn't left her clutch purse beside the sofa. Not that it had anything useful in it other than money and her keycard.

Something Lukas had said before reformed in her mind—about her family appreciating her loyalty—made her pause. She wasn't sure that Isabelle appreciated it as much as she took it for granted but an idea was taking shape.

If Lukas agreed to hire her as a consultant for his project and would form a partnership with Harrington's, then Isabelle would be forced to sit up and take notice of her achievements. And she had no doubt, given Lukas's passion for the project, his budget would be huge.

Would Isabelle go for the idea?

Eleanore chewed on her lower lip. She might dislike Lukas Kuznetskov, but as he had said to her, *business was business*, and she was pretty sure Isabelle would see it the same way. And the opportunities were obvious.

This would be Harrington's first hotel in Eastern Europe. A foot in the door to another market with zero capital outlay up front. It was like a gift, but a conditional one, because it came with Lukas Kuznetskov attached.

Could she work with a man she found so incredibly attractive and resist him? Eleanore scoffed at her reflection. Well, of course she could.

CHAPTER THREE

'A PARTNERSHIP?'

Lukas felt his eyebrows climb his forehead. Was the woman crazy? He'd never had a partner in his life. Not that he didn't admire her chutzpah in putting the idea to him.

She had guts, and he admired that in a person. 'And you think I'm an opportunist?' he quipped.

'I didn't say that.'

He smiled at her quick back step. 'First I get the brush-off tune and now I get the suck-up tune. I can't wait to see what comes next. Will it be the seduction tune?' Not that he wanted that...

'Listen, Mr Kuznetskov.' She planted her hands on her slender hips. 'I haven't changed my tune at all. I said you were self-important and obnoxious and comments like that only confirm my view.'

He studied her in her crumpled dress and

face free of make-up, her hair pulled back neatly once again. She had the most translucent skin he had ever seen and his fingers itched to trace over her face to see if it was as soft as it appeared. He wondered if she had any idea that standing before him all riled and cranky made him want to channel all that pent-up energy into another activity. One that involved her naked on the carpeted floor and him buried deeply between her soft thighs. All the blood in his body surged south at the idea and it took some effort to force it to return to his brain.

With time running out what he needed to do right now was get Eleanore Harrington's expertise and knowledge to complete his ice hotel, not be thinking about how her breasts would feel in the palms of his hands.

'I don't do partners.' But he did do money and in accordance with that he named a figure to procure her services that even a pampered heiress would find difficult to refuse.

She blinked her pretty eyes at him a couple of times and he wondered if he'd just found the golden key to securing her cooperation.

'I take it that's the fee you're offering me to take on the most impossible job on the planet?'

Lukas told himself to forget about whether her eyes were more green or more gold. 'If it was that impossible,' he quipped, 'you wouldn't have suggested being a partner in it.'

She smiled. 'Touché, Mr Kuznetskov, but I do think it's impossible. Well...' She bit into her plump bottom lip. 'Almost impossible. But I don't want your money. I want Harrington's name above the front door.'

He paused. Had he really just heard her right? 'No way.'

She shrugged as if that was that. 'Then I'm not interested.'

'You forget,' he said, relaxing his posture, 'there are other contenders out there.'

'I haven't forgotten that,' she returned coolly, 'but I know you're desperate and you won't find anyone else as good as me.'

She held one hand behind her back and he wondered if she didn't have her fingers crossed. Regardless, she was right about how desperate he was.

'Touché yourself, Eleanore.'

She smiled like a woman who held all the aces. And with her haughty nose raised in the air at him and her curvy little body, maybe she did. How he had ever thought her marginally pretty was beyond him. She was so much more than that in the flesh. Warm, sparkling and...feisty. An alluring combination of intellect and innocence he found strangely appealing. Not that any of that meant he'd give in to her request. She was about to find out that a willingness to compromise was not one of his stronger traits. 'Why do you want Harrington's name on the door?'

'Because I'm a Harrington and it will be my designs you use.'

'It's my hotel.'

'It's your money putting up the hotel, yes, but if you use my designs, then conceptually it's equally mine.'

Lukas scoffed. 'Equally? I don't think so.'

'But you do need me. You said so yourself.'

As much as he admired her sassy comeback he wasn't going to give in on this. And he knew she was more interested in working on his hotel than she was letting on. 'Maybe it's *you* who needs *me*.'

Her eyes cut to his, wide and wary. 'What do you mean?'

'You've thought about this hotel a lot since I mentioned it, have you not?'

She wasn't happy with his question; he could see that in the tightening of her mouth. She shrugged as if trying to act casually but it was too late. When you dragged yourself up from the dirtiest streets in the world to become one of the wealthiest men in it, you learned a fair bit about how to read people and Eleanore was a babe in arms when it came to negotiating. Not that he wasn't enjoying sparring with her. In fact, he couldn't remember the last time he'd been so invigorated by a woman's intellect instead of her body.

She arched her brow. 'Not as much as you,' she parried.

'Tell me,' he asked softly, 'who else is ever going to give you an opportunity to spread your wings on such an interesting project?'

She lifted her chin. 'My sister.'

Lukas doubted Harrington's could afford the spend. He smiled. 'Who is presently tied up battling the Chatsfields for control of your company from what I read last night. Why would I tie my business to such a circus?'

Her mouth flattened even more. 'Harrington's is not a circus and if you think that horrible Spencer Chatsfield will succeed in taking over our business, then you don't know my sister very well.'

'Actually, I don't know her at all but irrespective of who controls Harrington's at the end of the day your sister doesn't have the finances to put up a hotel like the Krystal Palace.'

Eleanore wrinkled her pretty little nose at him and he knew he'd guessed right. 'You have no idea if that's true or not.'

Lukas relaxed back in his chair and pushed his mobile phone toward her. 'Call her and ask. I doubt you could afford to pay for the front step after the amount spent on that bar last night.'

'That bar will pay for itself in time.'

Lukas held her hostile gaze and wondered if she wouldn't tell him to go to hell. He probably would if their positions were reversed.

'Come on, Eleanore,' he encouraged softly, 'come work for me. Harrington's name isn't worth that much any more.'

He could see immediately that he'd made a tactical error in reminding her of how he had inadvertently slurred her hotel chain once before.

'It is so worth something.' She practically vibrated out of her chair. 'It took my father years to establish a line of boutique hotels that are respected all over the world. Why do you think the Chatsfields want us so badly? We're a powerhouse and you should be thanking me for wanting to put our name on your hotel.'

Maybe he should and he wondered what it would feel like to have someone loyal to him as she obviously was to her family. What it would feel like to have all that passion wrapped tightly around him.

'And might I remind you,' she continued haughtily, 'that it was you who sought me out and told me you wanted my help. Well, it comes at a price. And I've just given it to you.' She stood up and his first thought was that she was magnificent in her wounded pride. His second was that he was sorry he'd somehow caused that and he was shocked by the realisation. Since when did he care about wounding an opponent's pride?

But Eleanore wasn't an opponent, was she? She was… He frowned. As much as he hated to admit it she was someone he needed. Oh, he was sure, given time, that he could find someone else who could pull off his ice hotel but time was something he had precious little of and she had made all the right suggestions so far. He shook his head. 'I'll take you on as a consultant, but not a partner.'

She muttered something under her breath— something he doubted was complimentary— before striding to his side and flipping his laptop around to face them both. 'Which one of these preliminary ideas did you like the most?' She sat down, stroking the mouse key and scrolling through the images until she came to a picture of the reception area. 'You know with very little effort we could turn these vaulted cathedral ceilings into glass domes that made them look like they touched the sky. But maybe you prefer the idea about the themed guest rooms. Off the top of my head my favourite would be the captain's quarters of an old-fashioned pirate ship with carved atlases and a four-poster bed. You might like a room with a Japanese infusion—ice futon and a tropical fish tank in the ceiling.'

'You can put a tropical fish tank in the ceiling?'

She straightened away from him, breathing hard, her eyes chips of green fire. 'I can do anything.'

Right now Lukas didn't doubt it.

And it wasn't often that he had been surprised in his life—well, in his adult life. Or impressed.

He turned his head and caught a whiff of apples. If she turned her head toward him they would be inches apart and he had a sudden and very primitive urge to taste her.

As if sensing his thoughts she went still and then shifted very subtly away from him. Harnessing a driving need to follow he clamped down on his unusually wayward libido and forced himself to relax back against the sofa. 'Actually, I quite like the sound of that pirate's cabin.'

She flushed a tempting shade of pink and twisted to face him, her deep breaths pushing her plump breasts forcefully against the front of her dress. 'Is that a *yes* to my conditions?'

He ignored the unhelpfully explicit instructions from his body and forced his mind to concentrate on the conversation before he gave her the hotel and his shipping business along with it. 'Not to putting Harrington's name on the door but I will put your name on the promotional material.'

She frowned at him and worried her bottom lip with her even white teeth. 'Does that include the website and all related online media as well as brochures?'

'As the designer only.'

'Creator.'

'It's my concept.'

'Soon to be *our* concept.' A genuine smile cracked across her face and Lukas felt his heart miss a beat—as impossible as that was to have actually occurred—and he found himself agreeing before he'd meant to. Another surprise he'd prefer not to think too deeply about. 'You can have your "Creation by Harrington's" but it's my hotel and all your decisions go through me, is that understood?'

If possible her smile widened. 'Of course.' She held out her hand for him to shake.

Lukas paused before taking it, a strange feeling his life was about to change and not necessarily for the better. Then he enfolded her fine-boned hand in his and wondered why it was he couldn't shake the desire to have her in his bed.

'How soon can you be ready to fly out to St Petersburg?'

She blinked. 'Now?'

'You were the one who told me my time line was optimistic.'

'Yes, well, I need a shower first.' She got up from the sofa, collected her bag and stopped. 'Oh, no.'

Distracted by her legs, Lukas flicked her an annoyed glance. 'Oh, no—what?'

'Oh, no, I just remembered whose hotel I'm in.' She crinkled her nose. 'Couldn't you have stayed somewhere else?'

'My PA booked the hotel. I quite like it.'

She looked less than impressed with his response and he was surprised to find that his mind was still on sex and now sex in the shower. A pointless endeavour when he had no intention of confusing his professional interest in her with a personal one. 'Go. I'll pick you up in an hour.'

'Before I do.' She turned back from the door and Lukas gritted his teeth. 'What's the temperature in St Petersburg?'

'Cold.' Just like him.

CHAPTER FOUR

HE WASN'T JOKING, Eleanore thought as she stood in the open doorway of Lukas's private plane and looked down on the snow-covered tarmac.

But cold wasn't exactly the word she would use. No, she'd tend more toward the word *freezing*. Maybe frigid. Or arctic…

She huddled further into her puffer jacket that did little to stop the cold from seeping through to the business suit she'd changed into prior to landing. She noticed that Lukas seemed impervious to the weather. Well, he would, she supposed; he'd grown up here and he had that big black cloak thingy on his wide shoulders again.

'You weren't being flippant when you said it would be cold,' she murmured, feeling as if all the air was being punched out of her lungs every time she took a breath.

He turned to her. 'I thought a New Yorker would be used to the cold.'

'So did I.' She shivered and zipped her normally adequate jacket right up to her chin. 'But this is something else altogether. How cold is it?'

'About minus twenty-seven.'

'Oh, good grief.'

Glad when they reached the warmth of Lukas's limousine she slid gratefully into the soft seats and let out a relieved sigh when he pulled the door closed.

Lukas, of course, seemed to find her condition utterly amusing and Eleanore kept her eyes glued to the scenery outside the window as the car carried them into town, all her senses riveted to the wide streets and beautiful ornate buildings, some capped with the famed gold onion domes renowned throughout Russia. It was like a winter wonderland.

A group of skaters caught her attention. 'What are those people ice skating on? The sidewalks?'

'Mostly the canals. St Petersburg is built on a network of islands and the water freezes solid in winter. I take it you like ice skating.'

'Not at all.' She grimaced and shook her head. 'Sport was never my thing. Olivia is sensational at it though.'

'And Olivia is?'

'My other sister. She's an actress.'

'A talented family.'

Eleanore glanced outside the window again because while she knew she was good at her job she was not in either of her sisters' league.

Not wanting to brood over things she couldn't change she let herself become lost in the retail sector that flashed past her window as they neared the centre of town. Some of the brand names she recognised as coming from any cosmopolitan city, but others bore exotic Russian names that were impossible for her to pronounce.

Pedestrians dotted the sidewalks clad in long thick coats with their collars turned up and enormous hats on their heads. 'I had no idea St Petersburg was so beautiful,' she said, awed by the graceful, wintery landscape.

'It's deceptive,' Lukas said curtly. 'And it's far from a winter wonderland, believe me.'

He sounded so emphatic she cut her gaze back to his but he was staring down at his phone.

The view outside his window caught her attention and she gasped in delight as she took in the famous Palace Square.

Lukas looked up. 'You know it?'

'Who doesn't know it?' She felt a grin split across her face. 'It's considered an architectural masterpiece with its smooth corners and the way it's framed by the jade Winter Palace on one side and the General Staff Building on the other. And look, there's the double arch with the famous winged Goddess of Victory. You know that was a symbol of Russia's defeat of Napoleon? Oh, sorry.' She stopped when she noticed that he was staring at her as if she were an idiot. 'Of course you know all this. You grew up here.'

Lukas shook his head slowly. Her enthusiasm was infectious but it was clear by her wide-eyed wonder that she had never experienced the darker side of life. 'I know the Palace Square is right beside one of our main train stations that has heating all night long and that the winged goddess is a great meeting spot for certain…transactions.'

'Oh?' Her curious gaze returned to his. 'Do tell.'

Her eyes glowed with an inner fire that was mesmerising. An inner fire he did not want to think about or feed. 'Maybe another time.'

Like never.

'I look forward to it,' she said eagerly. 'One of the things I love about new places is the history that is reflected through the buildings. It's one of the reasons I took architecture in school. And I love hearing about a city from a local's point of view. You can learn so much. How do you pronounce the name on that building over there?'

Lukas told her and Eleanore shook her head. Languages had never been her forte but they intrigued her all the same. And so far she hadn't had any time to learn this one.

Deciding to look up the basics on the internet she nearly fainted when she saw the length of the word for hello. 'Is this right?' she asked Lukas, turning her iPad toward him. 'Is this really hello?'

He looked faintly amused at her outburst. '*Da*. Yes. But you don't have to worry about learning the language. Most of my employees speak English.'

'I'm not worried, but it's polite to greet someone in their own language.'

He considered her for longer than was comfortable and she struggled not to squirm under the weight of his striking gaze. She found it much easier to think when she wasn't looking at him. Or at least to think about things that didn't involve what he would look like without any clothes on.

'*Zdravstvuyte* is hello. *Dasvidaniya* is goodbye and *spasibo* is thank you.'

Determined not to find him at all attractive Eleanore ignored the glint of humour in his eyes.

Attractiveness was only mind over matter anyway.

'Informative,' she muttered, repeating the words in her head a few times before making a note on how to pronounce them on her iPad, which was when she remembered the list of questions she'd made during the flight. She pulled them up. 'You know now might be a good time to talk about the budget.'

'Big,' he said.

Holding his gaze she willed her cheeks not to redden as her mind went in an entirely inappropriate direction with that word.

'Right.' She moved to the next item on her list. 'And your target demographic?'

'Couples.'

She raised an eyebrow. 'Just couples? That seems a bit limiting.'

Lukas shrugged. 'The hotel isn't large enough to accommodate a varied market and it's my experience that you're better to focus on one area and do it well before expanding to incorporate other markets.'

Forced to agree with his assessment she made some notes and mulled over his comments. 'So you want romantic.'

'Sexy.'

She looked up. 'Excuse me?'

'Sex, Eleanore. I want the hotel to be elegant

and stylish and I want it to ooze sex appeal. You do know what I'm talking about, don't you, Miss Harrington?'

Eleanore hated the sardonic gleam in his eye. Of course she knew what it was. She was unfortunately looking at it right now.

So much for mind over matter.

Deciding to ignore his taunt, and her own spiraling thoughts, she strove for professionalism. 'The hotel has to be about more than that.'

'Why?'

'Why?' Was he being obtuse to push her buttons? 'Because relationships are about more than sex.'

'They are?'

Determined to ignore the mocking glint in his eye she pushed on. 'You know they are. They're about intimacy and friendship and fun.'

'Fun?' His frown spoke volumes and she recalled his reputation for short-term affairs. 'Surely you're not going to tell me you've never had fun with a woman?'

'I'm not going to tell you anything,' he grated, clearly annoyed with her. 'Other than what I already have.'

Eleanore mentally rolled her eyes and then forgot about Lukas as her attention was snagged by something outside the window. 'Is that a horse and cart?'

Lukas followed her line of sight. 'A sleigh.'

'Oh!' She laughed. 'Of course, that's what I meant.'

'I take it that excites you as well?'

The way he looked at her made her cheeks redden again. 'Yes, it does. I've never seen a real one before.' She watched the polished black sleigh with a couple snuggled up together in the back, a brightly coloured blanket thrown over their knees. The driver wore a big Russian hat and heavily embroidered jacket and with the graceful buildings iced with snow in the background the whole storybook scene was like something out of a Tolstoy novel.

She sighed. 'Now that, my friend, is romantic.'

His eyes fixed on her face in an inscrutable expression. 'But hardly sexy.'

The air between them stretched tight for the longest time until finally Lukas broke the searing connection by returning his attention to his phone.

Annoyed that she had once again been caught up in his animal magnetism while he had been completely unaffected Eleanore glanced back at the glossy sleigh passing a group of ice skaters. Romance was sexy and she'd prove it to him if it was the last thing she did.

'No.'

Eleanore frowned as Lukas strode into the cavernous foyer of his office building and headed for the bank of shiny elevators. He hadn't even heard the whole of her idea yet and already he'd dismissed it.

She wished he'd slow down. Even if she wasn't wearing heels she would need to take two steps to his one. And if he went slower it would give her time to take in the sheer wonder of his building. Steel, glass, mirror-finished dark floors, curves and angles. It was a feat of engineering elegance and she just wanted to stop and stare.

They stepped into a waiting lift and Lukas swiped his keycard across the security pad. A few more corporate heads joined them but Eleanore barely noticed. 'You haven't even heard all my ideas yet.'

'I don't have to. And I have already said that I want this hotel to be elegant and revolutionary and sexy, not some sort of fun park.'

Eleanore let out a long sigh. He was going to be as impossible to work with as she had first thought. 'I'm not intending to turn it into a fun park, but let's face it, if people are coming to Russia in the dead of winter they're going to want to do more than sit by the fire and drink vodka.'

'Yes, they're going to want to have sex.'

Eleanore briefly closed her eyes, determined to maintain a level of professionalism with him she usually had no trouble attaining. 'Didn't you say your target audience was couples?'

'Yes, and they're going to want to have *lots* of sex.'

Suddenly becoming conscious of their rapt audience Eleanore lowered her voice. 'They'll want lots of romance too, and sleigh rides and huskies pulling sleds are definitely romantic. And very Russian. And really, at some point your couples are going to get sick of all that bed time together and want to find something else to do.'

'If they get sick of *all that bed time*,' he murmured provocatively, 'then they're not doing it very well.'

'Maybe you should offer lessons,' she suggested tartly.

A smile flickered at one corner of his mouth and his eyes held hers. 'Maybe I should.'

Eleanore's breath caught and she deliberately cast her eyes around the small elevator at the frozen expressions on the other occupants' faces. She smiled at the woman beside her. '*Dasvida*—oh, I mean *zstraduetye*.' Even though she covered her slip she barely got a nod from the woman, or anyone else. Probably they were all as shocked by the topic of their conversation as she was.

The lift seemed to stop at every floor in the building but finally it was blessedly empty and she turned back to Lukas. 'You've certainly given those people something to talk about at the water cooler later on. You do realise everyone was staring at you when you mentioned sex.'

'On the contrary, everyone was staring at you because you were challenging me.'

'Why? Don't people usually challenge you?'

Not like she did. Which wasn't the most comfortable of realisations. It made him feel as if the balance of power in his carefully constructed world was somehow under threat. An illogical thought because the petite woman beside him was about as dangerous as a daisy. 'No.'

'Well, that seems silly. Surely they don't agree with everything you say.'

Irritation at her persistence rode him hard. 'If they don't they table their concerns in the appropriate manner and then they'd better have a damned good reason for wasting my time with it.'

Eleanore frowned up at him. 'But how do you build on your ideas? How do you flesh them out?'

'My ideas rarely need fleshing out. They just need executing.'

'Oh, right. You and Stalin both.'

Her soft mouth twitched with humour and Lukas wondered what she would do if he gave in to his body's urges and leant forward and kissed her. Would she resist or would she melt like butter in the hot sun? He recalled her assertion moments ago that relationships were about more than sex. That they were about fun, and he was annoyed to realise that he couldn't remember the last time he'd had fun. And fun with a woman? The type she was talking about. Did that even exist?

Wanting to quash the unsettled feelings in the pit of his stomach he pointed his finger at her. 'No sleigh rides, no huskies and sleds, and—' the lift doors pinged open '—no reindeers with red noses either.'

A mutinous scowl crossed her face and she raised her chin as she stalked out of the lift ahead of him. Something else people around him tended not to do. When she gasped in awe at the layout of his private sanctuary something deeply satisfying bloomed in his chest.

'I love these plants. They're gorgeous. And incredibly hard to grow.'

Plants? What plants? Lukas ran his gaze around the room and saw a corner filled with green palm fronds. Had they always been there?

'I love the use of the space as well and the angle of the windows. Is that because they have solar panels attached to the bottom?' She strode over to peer outside.

'Yes. I wanted the building to be self-sustaining.'

She glanced over her shoulder at him. 'This was your idea?'

He didn't like the amazement that flashed across her face as if somehow he was too base to consider environmental concerns. Especially when he'd commissioned the solar panels before it had become trendy to do so. 'It's my building, who else's would it be? Stalin's?'

Her mouth kicked up a little. 'Well, as much as it pains me to admit it, I like it.'

'I'm so very pleased to have your endorsement, Miss Harrington,' he said sarcastically, irritated to find that actually he was. It wasn't as if he sought out, or desired, anyone's approval, let alone a woman who looked far too good in a pencil skirt.

She smiled at something behind him and crossed the room. *'Zdrasvustske.'*

Lukas grimaced at her appalling pronunciation and turned to see her holding her hand out to his PA. 'I'm Eleanore Harrington.'

His usually self-contained assistant, who saw herself more and more as a mother figure in his life the longer they worked together, seemed almost stunned to be faced with the exuberant Eleanore Harrington. 'I'm Petra. Lukas's PA.'

'It's nice to meet you, Petra.'

His assistant cut her eyes to his, sparkling merrily. 'Lukas, you have a mountain of work on your desk. I've been through most of your messages for this morning and prioritised them for you with notes attached. Also, your meeting schedule for tomorrow has been sent to your phone. Sorry it's late. I was waiting to hear back from the bank before confirming it.'

'Thank you, Petra. If you wouldn't mind organising coffee. Miss Harrington has hers white with one sugar.'

'Oh, that's okay,' Eleanore said quickly. 'I don't feel like coffee right now and you sound like you have a lot to catch up on.'

Lukas frowned. Was he being dismissed? 'When can I see the drawings you spent the whole flight working on?' And why did he sound like a petulant child when he should have been glad she had so easily blocked him out during the long flight?

She pulled a face. 'They're not ready for public consumption yet. I still need to walk around the site before I finalise anything. Didn't you organise a site visit for this afternoon?'

'Yes. My foreman will meet you there and tomorrow morning you will meet the rest of the team.'

'Great. Then if you wouldn't mind showing me where I'm to work I'll go prepare for it.'

'It's right this way,' his PA cut in, and Lukas realised that hell yes, he was being dismissed. And he didn't like it.

Eleanore connected with Petra's matronly, down-to-earth friendliness right away. And she really liked the office she'd been assigned. 'Oh, I have a view.' She stared out the window at the elegant snow-covered city below. In New York her view was of a rusty fire escape on the high-rise directly opposite.

'Mr Kuznetskov wanted all the offices to have a view,' Petra began in her heavily accented voice, 'and as we are the tallest building in the district he accomplished it.'

'You like working for him.'

'I love it.'

For some reason that surprised Eleanore but maybe Petra was just blind to his faults. She glanced around at the neat office and noticed a large white box on her desk. 'I think someone might have left something in the office.'

'No, that's a coat, hat and gloves. Lukas asked me to arrange it before you left Singapore.'

'That was very thoughtful of him,' she said, wondering why he would do such a thing.

Inside she found a lovely black jacket lined with real fur. Something that meant she would never be able to wear it.

'I know.' Petra pulled open a drawer and started setting up the desk for her. 'He's always thinking of others.'

'He is?' Was this the same man who was known in the press for his ruthless takeover of smaller companies and who went through women the way florists went through rosebuds?

'Oh, yes. When my mother needed surgery for a bad fall last year we couldn't afford it and he helped out by providing a nurse for three months. And of course this ice hotel is for charity.'

'Charity?' That was news to her.

'Did he not tell you?'

'No.' And then she wondered if maybe there was a language barrier and *charity* didn't mean the same as it did in America. 'Are you sure?'

Petra gave her a funny look. 'Of course I'm sure. And last year he opened a crèche at the office for the parents who were struggling with child care.'

'I did that,' the man himself drawled from the office doorway, startling both her and his PA, 'so that my employees wouldn't waste time commuting and worrying about their children. It was efficient.'

Now that made sense to what Eleanore knew of him.

Petra gave Eleanore a don't-believe-him look. 'The staff loved you for it.'

'Then it was worth every penny. And speaking of staff, a few of the key people you need to meet have to leave the building site early today so we need to get moving now.'

Eleanore pinned a smile on her face when she realised he was coming with her. 'You're coming too?'

'*Da*. Is that a problem?'

Yes. After a long flight where she'd struggled to concentrate on work she needed some time away from him. 'Of course not,' she said pleasantly, more for Petra's benefit than for his.

'Good. Grab the jacket and we'll go.'

'I can't.'

'It doesn't fit?'

Petra beamed a smile at him. 'She hasn't tried it on yet.'

Eleanore trained her gaze on Lukas and wondered how she was going to get around not wearing the jacket without offending Petra, who had obviously chosen it. 'Um…'

'Give us a moment, would you, Petra?'

'Sure. I'll be in my office if you need me.'

Lukas waited for her to pass before strolling further into the office. He'd rolled his shirt-sleeves to his elbows again and Eleanore really wished he wouldn't do that.

'What is it now?' he asked silkily.

For some reason Eleanore felt terrible rejecting the jacket. 'It was a nice gesture but I can't wear it.'

'It wasn't a nice gesture,' he said in a bored voice. 'It was efficient. If you come down with an illness you'll be useless to me. Now stop trying to be contrary and go and put it on.'

'I'm not trying to be contrary.' She picked up her puffer jacket from the back of the office chair and slid her arms into the sleeves. 'I already have a jacket.'

'You have a *New York* jacket that works in temperatures not exceeding minus ten. By the time you finish the site visit wearing that you'll be frozen solid.'

'Well, I can't wear this one. I have a thing about fur.'

'Want to run that by me again?'

'It has fur on it. Real fur. Have you heard of PETA?'

'Is he a lover who doesn't like fur?'

'No, it's an organisation that supports the ethical treatment of animals.'

Half expecting him to tell her she was being ridiculous she was surprised when he only released a weary breath and jerked away from the doorway. 'Let's go.'

CHAPTER FIVE

'THIS WASN'T MEANT to be a fashion stopover,' Lukas growled, glancing at the time on his phone.

'It's not that easy to decide,' Eleanore told him from in front of the store mirror.

It was for him.

One overcoat was as good as another as far as he was concerned. And frankly every time she shrugged out of one to put on the next her suit jacket opened wide and her silk blouse pulled tight across the tips of her breasts, outlining her lacy bra beneath. Did nobody else notice that but him?

'Just pick one,' he ordered, 'or I'll do it for you.'

Both Eleanore and the salesgirl looked at him as if he was mad. He felt mad.

'*Bozhe*, it's just a jacket!'

'I don't like wearing clothes I don't love.'

His eyes narrowed. Was she for real? 'Clothes are clothes.' Although even as he said it he knew that wasn't true. Clothes had a way of defining who you were, not that he really gave a damn personally, but those with money only wanted to mix with other people with money. It was the law of the social jungle.

'So says the man with the custom-made shoes.'

Of course she'd noticed. She was from old money. She'd no doubt marry someone one day who was from old money and together they'd have lovely children with perfect pedigrees. *And could his thoughts become any more pointless?*

With a growl he rose from the ruby-red chaise and riffled through a rack of overcoats. He stopped at an olive-green cashmere coat and yanked it off the hanger. It was lined with a quilted fabric printed with rows of brightly coloured exotic birds that reminded him of her. Since it looked about the right size he marched behind her and held it up. 'Put this on.'

Her eyes caught his in the mirror just as they had the night before in the ice bar and again he felt an unexplainable jolt somewhere in the vicinity of his solar plexus. Annoyed he shook the coat. 'Any time this year will be good, Miss Harrington.'

'Oh, right.' Her long lashes swept down to cover her fascinating eyes and his groin tightened even more when she fitted first one arm and then the other into the coat.

'Oh, it's gorgeous.'

Lukas didn't bother looking. He already knew the green would bring out the same tones in her eyes. He grabbed an *ushanka* from a hat stand and checked the tag. Fur. He went through five more before he found one she wouldn't be offended with. It was black and soft and had ear flaps. Then he chose gloves and a muff and returned to her.

'I can't put that on my head. It will ruin my hairdo.'

'Take it down.'

'Take it down?'

She stared at him in the mirror again, the green jacket totally encompassing her from neck to calf, and Lukas didn't think he'd been more turned on in his life. This was supposed to have been a two-minute stopover to ensure that she didn't fall ill from being underdressed and instead he was watching as she raised her arms to release her hair and he was riveted to the spot like a store mannequin. The chestnut waves fell about her shoulders in a cloud of silken strands and the scent of fresh apples rose to his nose. Her cheeks were flushed as she gazed at his reflection and it was all he could do not to spin her around and crush her pink lips beneath his own.

He glanced up at the heating vents in the high ceilings and wondered if someone had just turned the furnace up to full bore. It was so hot it almost seemed redundant to dump the *ushanka* on her head but he did it anyway.

'Ouch.'

She raised her hand to adjust the hat and he shoved the gloves into her hand. 'No fur, so don't complain.'

'I'm not complaining.'

She moved toward the small fitting room to look at herself more closely. Lukas turned away.

'Put that on my account,' he told the boggle-eyed salesgirl.

'Yes, sir.'

'No, wait. I'm paying.'

Eleanore grabbed her purse and spun around to rush out of the sitting room except that Lukas was in her way.

She stopped, startled at how close he was. 'I mean it, Mr Kuznetskov. I don't need you to buy clothes for me.'

No, she wouldn't need anything from him, Lukas thought, and why did that realisation make him more annoyed. 'This isn't about what *you* need, Miss Harrington, it's about what *I* need.' And he really needed to get out of this ridiculously hot store.

'I can buy my own clothes.'

'This is a business expense.'

She frowned. 'Can you do that?'

He had no idea and he didn't care. 'I can do whatever I want.'

'I think you've been doing whatever you want for far too long.'

Eleanore hadn't actually meant to blurt out her thoughts like that but somehow he drove her to say things she would normally keep to herself.

'True.'

His offhand reply riled her, especially after Petra's earlier revelations about his do-gooding deeds had made her think she had read his character wrong. 'And what's this about the proceeds of the ice hotel going to a charity?'

Something in his expression became guarded. 'What about it?'

'If Harrington's is to be associated with the hotel I feel like it's something we should have known about already.'

'And now you do.'

Frustrated with his unconcerned attitude she scowled up at him and tried to ignore the feeling of being trapped. 'Which charity is it?'

He shrugged. 'I can't remember.'

'You can't remember?'

'That's what I said.'

Eleanore frowned. 'So why do it?'

'Because I can.'

Maybe she hadn't got him wrong after all. Maybe Petra was just hoodwinked. 'And no doubt looking good in the community doesn't hurt either,' she said.

It aggravated him that she had already pegged him as a bad person after one comment that hadn't been meant for public consumption. It was as if she could see the very essence of him and knew there was something lacking inside of him. 'There is that,' he agreed flatly.

The way she gripped her handbag to her chest and glared at him let him know she was ready to leave but he ignored the cue.

'If possible I think my opinion of you just sunk lower,' she said snootily.

'Is that something I'm supposed to care about?' he asked.

'Obviously not.'

Her haughty attitude was like nails down a chalkboard to his soul and Lukas's irritation spilled over. Who was she to judge him? 'Are you quite finished with the interrogation?' he bit out tersely. 'We have a month to turn this project around and I need someone competent and willing to work hard.'

Her chin jerked upward. 'Why do I feel like you just slighted me?'

'Perhaps my opinion of you isn't that much higher than your opinion of me.'

'We should make a great team, then,' she said testily.

Lukas stepped into the doorway of her dressing cubicle. 'We're not a team, Miss Harrington. I've hired you to work on a project for my company.'

'Well, exsqueeze me.'

'Pardon?'

'Nothing.' She didn't know why she felt stung by his words but she did. 'You know there's something just so damned attractive about a man without a sense of humour who is doing something altruistically and doesn't give a damn.'

Lukas raised both arms and placed his hands on top of the cubicle doorframe and leaned toward her. 'But I'm not trying to be attractive,' he said softly.

Eleanore produced a smile worthy of a jackpot winner. 'Oh, to be as successful as you are,' she challenged.

His eyes grew hooded as he studied her and Eleanore had to resist the urge to fidget under his intrusive gaze. She knew she was digging at him to cover her awareness of him.

An awareness she did not want to feel given that she didn't even like the man or his seeming lack of values. 'You have a smart mouth.'

He stared at said smart mouth and she felt her lips tingle. She held perfectly still as if she were a small field mouse waiting for the big tom cat to spring. As if she *wanted* the big tom cat to spring. 'Perhaps it needs to be put to better use.'

It took a moment for his remark to register and when it did Eleanore had no idea how to respond. Her mind was fuddled by the heat radiating from his body as he towered over her and it took everything she had just to resist leaning in close enough to touch him. Shocked by a yearning she hadn't felt before she arched a brow as if she dealt with situations like this all the time.

'Eating?' she suggested, trying for lightness but knowing she'd missed by a wide margin when he smiled a slow smile that spoke of pleasure the likes of which she had never known before.

'Of a sort.'

She took in a slow breath and reminded herself that he was a rampant male chauvinist who had obviously gotten his way for far too long.

'Or is that what you want, Eleanore?'

The way he said her name—deliberately low

and gruff—sent a spill of liquid heat through her pelvis. 'What I want?' Somehow she had completely lost the thread of the conversation in the small confines of the cubicle, the heavy, unexpected throb of arousal absorbing her focus.

'Is all this arguing some sort of foreplay?'

Foreplay! The mere suggestion told her that he knew how much he affected her and she stiffened with raw embarrassment. She pulled the hat from her head, denial hot on her lips. 'I tend to *like* the men I engage in foreplay with.' She said it breezily, as if it was a daily occurrence.

'Then perhaps you're missing out. Perhaps you need to engage with someone you feel *passionate* about rather than someone you merely *like.*'

Eleanore swallowed heavily. 'Well, I can assure you that person is not you.' But even as she said the words she knew they were a lie. Since he'd walked up to her at Glaciers she had been totally aware of him as a virile male in the prime of his life. It was all she could do to concentrate on anything else.

He lowered his arms and stepped into her space, but she refused to look up at him, instead she kept her eyes on the open top button of his dress shirt.

'I've always been partial to apples,' he said roughly.

Apples? Her eyes flicked to his in surprise. Why was he talking about fruit when all she could think about was how close they were and how if she moved barely an inch the tips of her aching breasts would find some relief pressed up against the hard wall of his chest?

As if he could sense the inner turmoil of her mind fighting her body he lowered his head even further and spoke softly into her ear. 'Tell me what you want, *moya krasavitsa*.'

Tell him... Eleanore released a shaky breath. She didn't know what she wanted. Or she did but she didn't want it with *him*. Or anyone. Relationships were way down on her list of goals and she knew she couldn't afford to be distracted at a time when she was trying so hard to impress her sister with her professional abilities.

'I don't want anything from you,' she said shakily.

'Excuse me, Mr Kuznetskov, will that be all today?'

The salesgirl's interruption was such a welcome relief Eleanore expelled a rushed breath. 'Yes,' she said before Lukas could reply, 'and I'm paying.'

Much to her consternation the girl's eyes

darted to Lukas as if seeking his permission, which made Eleanore's temper soar. Women bowing down to him was the last thing a man like Lukas Kuznetskov needed.

She glared up at him and dared him to argue with her.

He studied her for a moment longer without moving and then he stepped to the side. 'By all means, Miss Harrington. Would you like her to stamp your feminist card as well?'

'Only if she'll stamp your chauvinistic one at the same time,' she said smartly.

He laughed softly and she ignored him, turning to slip past him, determined to show him how little he affected her. Unfortunately the room was a lot smaller than she realised and she drew in a sharp breath as her bottom brushed up against his thighs. It shouldn't have had any effect given the layers of clothing between them but streaks of tingling awareness zipped through her already aroused body and she had the overwhelming urge to push back against him.

His hands rose to rest lightly at her waist and she thought she heard him take a quick indrawn breath before she turned her head and saw the way he was staring at the spill of her hair down her back.

He looked at her as if he was about to bend

his head toward the creamy expanse of her neck, as if he was about to raise his hands and bring them around to cover her breasts that felt twice as full as normal, and for all her hot-headed denial she knew she wanted to feel what it would be like to have his hands on her. His mouth. Then he flashed his cocky movie star smile as if he knew exactly what she was thinking and she jerked back from him.

God, she was really starting to hate that smile.

Two hours later and dead on her feet Eleanore was relieved when Lukas's limousine pulled up outside what must be her apartment building.

All she could think about was a long shower or bath followed by a blissful night's sleep. She wasn't even sure she'd eat anything. Particularly since she had no idea how to order take-out in Russian and she didn't have the energy to find a local grocer to buy food.

And it would be such a relief to be away from Lukas and his disturbing presence as well. No matter how many times she told herself to think professionally, or reminded herself that he really was a cold, heartless business-man who had basically blackmailed her into working for him with his threats about going to the Chatsfields, she couldn't stamp out her sexual awareness of the man. Nor could she wipe out the feel of his hands on her waist or forget how intensely feminine she had felt pressed up against him. How much she had wanted to kiss him.

Was that even normal?

'No need to see me up,' she said a little too quickly, convinced that a good night's sleep would set her internal system back to right. 'Just tell me the number of the apartment and I'm sure I can find it easily enough.'

'And drive your opinion of me even lower by being inhospitable?'

Before she could stop herself Eleanore smiled sweetly. 'Please be reassured that it couldn't get any lower.'

His blue eyes dropped to her mouth and she wished that she'd held her tongue. Previously she would have said she didn't have a sarcastic bone in her body but somehow her parents' well-mannered training flew out the window when she was with this man.

'More foreplay, *moya krasavitsa*?'

Oh! Eleanore forced her jaw to unlock. 'I hope that's not something sexist you're calling me.'

His devilish smile encouraged her to push him for an answer. Instead she gave him a look before stepping out of the car.

When he followed her out she decided that the quickest way to a hot bath and a warm bed was to let him have his own way. She shook her head as if he was unredeemable and raised her chin as she moved past him.

The building was a butter-yellow neoclassical style and the inside was full of old-world glamour with mirrored surfaces and marble floors that warmed her soul. The apartment was on the fifth floor, and as it was with many old buildings the elevator was incredibly small. Wedging herself into a corner she stared at Lukas's shiny black shoes so that she wouldn't be tempted to stare at the man himself. She loved shoes and she knew his had been custom-made. Along with his suits, because no way could store-bought pants fit so perfectly that they gave a hint at the strength of his thighs but didn't cling in an ugly way as some men's did. He had his hands in his pockets so the sides of his suit jacket were pushed wide and it pulled his pants low on his lean hips, outlining... her heart bumped inside her chest. *Shoes*. She had been looking at his shoes. The expensive stitching, the...

The slight jerk of the lift as it shuddered to a stop brought a rushed exhalation of relief. Nearly there. Nearly out of her suddenly restrictive suit and maybe she had a rogue chocolate bar in her handbag she hadn't already inhaled at some point.

Hoping there would be a cup of tea inside the apartment with her name on it she followed Lukas out of the lift. When he stopped at the end of the hallway she was so caught up in her haste to end the day she barely managed not to barrel into the back of him. She gave him a brief smile and held her hand out for the apartment key.

Instead of handing it to her he unlocked the door. 'The apartment is serviced and used by travelling employees so you should find it has everything you need.'

Not about to be accused of wanting to engage in foreplay with him again she gave him a serene smile. 'Thanks. I'm sure it will be fine.'

Grunting something under his breath he headed inside the apartment and Eleanore had little choice but to follow.

Focusing on the elegant decor and rich furnishings in the open-plan living area she busied herself by taking off her overcoat and hat. Unused to the heavy weight of her hair down she secured it into a quick bun, not caring how untidy it might look. 'The apartment looks lovely,' she said lightly, hoping he'd hear the silent *please leave* in her tone.

Of course he ignored it if he did and headed

for the kitchen. Eleanore glanced at the ceiling in search of divine intervention. Unfortunately she seemed to be all on her own with him.

'I've had the housekeeper stock the kitchen with basic food.' He opened the fridge and peered inside. 'Milk, eggs, cheese, bread.' He glanced back at her. 'Do you cook?'

'Yes.'

One dark blond brow climbed his forehead. 'Really?'

Eleanore gave him a look. 'Yes.'

'What do you cook?'

'I don't know. Omelettes, pasta, sometimes a casserole that my mother used to make for us when she was alive. I'm very good with arsenic too.' She smiled. 'Would you like to stay for supper?'

He flashed her an amused grin and opened one of the overhead cupboards. 'Tempting but I'll pass. What happened to your mother?'

Eleanore rarely talked about her mother and her throat clogged. 'She died of cancer.'

Lukas heard the soft vulnerability in Eleanore's voice and knew that it had been a difficult experience for her. He found himself wanting to make her feel better. 'I'm sorry to hear that.'

She shrugged and he didn't know if she was trying to block him out as she'd tried to do since he'd met her or if it was a self-protective gesture. 'It was a long time ago. I was only nine.'

'But you miss her.'

She seemed surprised by his observation but not as surprised as he was himself. He rarely involved himself in conversations about anyone's parents or their pasts. It opened up the opportunity for them to ask him questions he had no intention of answering.

'I don't know if I miss her as much as I wish she were still here. Particularly as I get older. There's so much I'd like to ask her and say to her. And I can only imagine that getting worse when I have kids of my own. What about you? Are your parents still alive?'

Lukas had no idea. 'No kids and no parents.'

'Oh.' Her big hazel eyes widened with empathy. 'I'm sorry to hear that.'

'What, that I don't have kids or that I don't have parents?'

Realising how bleak those words had sounded he slammed the cupboard door and told himself to leave. 'Through there is the bathroom and two bedrooms. One is set up as an office with a pull-out sofa.' He moved back toward the main door before he turned around. He looked back and found her staring at him with those wide, empathetic eyes he could drown in, her mouth soft and pink, beckoning him to come drink from it so that he could wash all his pain away. All his troubles.

All his troubles? All his pain?

Caught off guard by unexplainable emotions Lukas nearly walked out the door before he realised that he still held her apartment keys in his pocket. Unused to feeling so off balance he marched back toward her, trying to make light of his gaffe. 'You'll need these, I expect.'

'Oh, right. Sure. Just…you can just leave them on the counter.' The smile she gave him was wary and her eyes still held some sort of sympathy he knew in a heartbeat he could replace with lust. He thought of her curvy bottom against his groin earlier. All that fragrant hair tumbling down her back.

Physical arousal coursed through him, swift and unequivocal. His body wanted Eleanore Harrington even though his mind warned him not to go near her.

But goading her as he'd done all afternoon whenever she had annoyed him was one thing, following through by taking her into his bed was something else altogether, and he might have been able to follow through with that thought if she hadn't bent down to unzip her high-heeled boots and release a moan of pleasure as she did so.

She wasn't looking at him, or even putting on a performance as some of his past women would have done to get his attention, and perversely that seemed to affect him even more. What was it about her that drew him so strongly? And why analyze it? Sex was a normal part of life, a means of relaxation. It would be no different with her so why hold back? 'So what's on the agenda for tonight, Eleanore?' He found himself asking before his mind was fully sold on the idea. 'A hot bath or are you more a shower kind of girl?'

Himself, he could do it in either.

Her cheeks flushed prettily and he knew she was headed for one of them, and right now he didn't care if he'd never mixed business with pleasure before…he wanted to strip her naked and join her.

'I…' She cleared her throat. 'Bed, actually.'

Well, hell, he could be conventional as well. He smiled. 'Want me to turn down the sheets?'

'I beg your pardon?'

Her haughtiness just inflamed him more. She was so proper. So different from him. 'I said…'

'I heard you. And I think you should leave.'

He came toward her and saw her pulse flicker rapidly in the base of her neck. 'Let's not pretend, Eleanore. I know you feel the chemistry between us as keenly as I do.' She shifted her weight from one foot to the other and he wondered if she was turned on already. 'You want this.'

She let out a startled laugh. 'Well, no one could ever accuse you of having an unhealthy ego.'

Now that he'd said the words out loud, now that he'd acknowledged that there was something between them, all Lukas could think about was touching her. Tasting her. *Taking* her.

The fact that she wasn't his type and that he'd never come on to an employee before no longer seemed relevant. She wasn't a permanent employee anyway.

'But you're wrong.' She stared at him defiantly. 'I don't want you.'

He hadn't even realised he'd moved closer to her until her clipped words penetrated the lust-filled fog in his brain. He stopped barely a metre in front of her. He wondered what she would do if he took two more steps and backed her against the wall, pressed himself against her and let her feel what state she had put him in all day. 'Coward,' he baited softly.

Her eyes narrowed and she moved to put some distance between them. 'I'm not a coward. And I won't deny that I find you physically attractive—on some level—but I intend to see a shrink about that as soon as I get back to New York.'

Lukas laughed and wondered if it wasn't her sassy wit that attracted him as much as her mouth and her legs. Her pert breasts and her smoking eyes. 'Why not do something about it here?' he suggested.

'The language barrier,' she deadpanned. 'Your shrinks probably only speak Russian.'

'I have a better idea than a shrink.'

'I do too. It's called you leaving.'

Lukas knew he was stalking her as he stepped closer and forced her back against the wall but all he felt was a primal satisfaction that he affected her as much as she affected him.

A coil of her hair had come loose from her messy hairdo and he tucked it behind the small shell of her ear. He loved the feel of a woman's skin there. It was a good indication of how smooth the skin between her inner thighs would feel and Eleanore's skin was like the petal of a new rose in bloom. She trembled and he noticed that the green and amber flecks in her eyes seemed to glow with longing. The same hungry longing that was eating him up inside.

She watched him, her small pink tongue

darting out to moisten her lips as if in anticipation of his kiss.

He nearly chuckled when he saw it. For all her determination to deny how much she wanted him he was almost disappointed at how easy this was going to be in the end.

Sensing his hesitation her long lashes swept up and her gorgeous eyes connected with his. Something passed between them, something that made Lukas's breathing suddenly shallow, made his heart bump erratically inside his chest. 'No, I don't think I will kiss you,' he murmured, fighting to understand why his instincts insisted that she was a danger to him. She was just a woman. 'I think I'll wait for you to kiss me.'

She blinked her eyes rapidly as if she'd been under a spell, narrowing them into murderous slits as she processed his arrogance. She pushed away from him. 'Why don't you hold your breath while you do that?'

This time he did chuckle. He couldn't help himself. He'd laughed more in the past twenty-four hours than he had in years. Maybe ever. And had it really only been that long? He felt like he'd known her for ever. 'It's going to be interesting,' he mused as he breathed in the lingering scent of her apple blossom shampoo. 'Seeing how long you can hold out.'

She crossed the room with measured strides as if she wasn't furious with him. 'You really do have tickets on yourself, Mr Kuznetskov,' she said over her shoulder.

'Shall we cast a wager?'

She turned. 'I beg your pardon?'

'A wager. On who will kiss whom first.'

'You're mad.'

'Is that a yes?'

Lukas could hear the words coming out of his mouth and he couldn't quite believe them. She'd aggravated him with the way she so easily froze him out. With the way she treated him as if he wasn't worth bothering about. *Printsessa* and the *nishchiy*, he thought, and felt a muscle tick in his jaw. And the more she tried to mind her p's and q's with him, the more he wanted to run roughshod all over them.

'No, it is not a yes.'

'Why not?'

'I don't gamble.'

Neither did he. Not usually. 'Live a little,' he goaded.

His words were a little too close to Lulu's and Eleanore wondered if she had some sign pinned to her forehead that said Boring.

She picked up the electric kettle and carried it to the sink to fill it. 'I live just fine,' she snapped, knowing there wasn't anything he could offer her that would entice her to play such a stupid game with him. Not when she worked for him and it would be completely unprofessional. Heck, she could just envision Isabelle's disapproval already.

'How about if I kiss you first you can have Harrington's name above the door of the hotel?'

Eleanore stilled. Looked back at him. 'Are you serious?'

'Why not?'

She couldn't believe he would wager that. 'And what happens if I kiss you first?'

'Worried about your self-control, *moya krasavitsa*?'

She hated not knowing what he was calling her but she wouldn't lower herself to ask. Let him have his fun. Men and their egos.

Mr I'm-So-Irresistible was about to meet his match. Water from the tap ran over the top of the kettle, down her arm and soaked the sleeve of her blouse. Cursing under her breath she gave him a tight smile. 'Shall we say I get to shoot you afterward?'

'Another tempting offer but no.' He smiled and handed her a towel. 'If you kiss me first, sweet Eleanore, then you give yourself to me completely.'

The soft words made Eleanore's insides tumble like the clothes in a spin dryer—only twice as hot and twice as fast. She threw the towel in the sink and put the kettle back on the electric plate. She knew she'd be mad to take his bet but, oh, what would happen if she got to put Harrington's name above the door of the Krystal Palace?

'Tempted, Eleanore?' He reached around her and flicked the switch on the kettle she'd forgotten to depress. Eleanore glared at the kettle as if it had betrayed her in some way.

'Not by you,' she scoffed with more bravado than she felt. 'But why not?' She crossed her arms over her chest. 'You seem to be in the market to learn some more life lessons, Mr Kuznetskov—perhaps humility will be another one.'

'You forget,' he purred close to her ear as he took her palm and enfolded the apartment keys inside. 'I have yet to learn the first one.'

Bastard, Eleanore thought, and nearly yelled it at him as he swaggered out of her apartment as if he owned the world and her along with it.

CHAPTER SIX

SHE WAS NOT dressing for him, Eleanore told herself as she threw yet another skirt from her suitcase onto the bed. But of course she was. She was dressing to tempt Lukas Kuznetskov into losing his schoolyard bet even though she'd woken with every intention of calling it off!

She spied the riot of clothes on her bed and huffed out a sigh. She'd done quite a bit of shopping during her weeks in Singapore but do you think she could come up with something suitable to wear?

The problem was that although she had some very sensible work suits and tops she hadn't bought anything with seduction in mind. And probably she should have unpacked last night instead of wasting so much time in the bath hating the man in question before falling into a restless sleep because what she did have was now full of wrinkles.

What she needed was something professional and yet subtly sexy but nothing jumped out at her. Then she spied the flirty little top Olivia had given her for Christmas the year before. It was hardly subtle and wasn't something she would usually pair with a suit because it was quite low-cut and didn't accommodate a bra.

She picked it up and held it in front of her. Olivia had said that going braless was the point and that the gold colouring made her eyes glow. Eleanore eyed her reflection dubiously. Maybe if she teamed it with a floaty scarf and kept her suit jacket buttoned, then no one would know.

Doesn't that defeat the purpose of wearing it, Eleanore?

Yes, but she was no femme fatale and maybe Lukas would somehow get a hint of it and be turned on anyway.

An image of how he had looked at her when he'd told her to take her hair down in the department store drifted into her consciousness. His eyes had gone from sapphire blue to almost navy and she'd felt the kick of the chemistry between them as strongly as a short black laced with sugar.

She knew he was attracted to her. He would just never be serious about her. But that was okay. She didn't plan to marry the man. Heck, she didn't even plan to sleep with him. She would just entice him to kiss her and win the bet.

On the verge of calling Olivia for some pointers on flirting, Eleanore changed her mind. Her sister would only want to know all the details and she didn't want word to get back to Isabelle, who would no doubt think her behaviour highly inappropriate. On that note Eleanore pulled up short. If Isabelle ever found out about the bet would she wonder if Lukas hadn't given her the contract because he was interested in her personally instead of professionally?

Given that Isabelle hadn't been that enthused about the project until Eleanore had mentioned that Lukas might have gone to the Chatsfields next she didn't want to give her sister any reason to doubt her competence on the project. Her nose crinkled as she thought about that. Isabelle was a stickler for doing the right thing; it came with being the eldest and running the family company, no doubt, and Eleanore would never do anything to jeopardise the promotion she was desperate to get but…she also couldn't deny the tiny thrill that zipped through her at the thought of pitting herself against Lukas Kuznetskov and winning. The man was just so full of himself and her sister need never know about how she'd won the right to have Harrington's name on the door and she was positive Lukas would never admit to losing a bet with a woman. He didn't seem the type.

No, it would be fine. She would win and have an even bigger coup to offer Isabelle than just finishing his spectacular hotel. A grin split across her face as she pulled the silky top over her head. She could barely wait for it to happen just to see the look on his face when she won.

'You don't play fair, Eleanore,' Lukas murmured as she took a seat beside him at the conference table.

'What are you talking about?' she asked, darting him a nervous look before pulling as far back in her seat as possible without toppling over.

When he'd arrived at the early-morning meeting she'd been talking with Greg Drummond, the site foreman he'd introduced her to the previous afternoon. Lukas hadn't like the way Drummond had looked at her then and he didn't like the way he was looking at her now.

His foreman's attention was just a little too tuned, his laughter just a little too enthusiastic. Still, it didn't mean that just because a man looked at a woman's legs with a glint in his eyes that he was planning to sleep with her.

Well…sometimes it did, but dammit, who was to say Eleanore was even Drummond's type? Yes, she had a great body her tight skirt and fitted suit jacket did little to hide and a pretty face and incredible eyes with dark silky lashes, but that didn't mean Drummond wanted her.

Lukas frowned. But nor did he need Drummond turning into some sort of lapdog for a month and becoming so distracted it jeopardised the completion of his hotel.

A feeling of jealousy he'd never experienced before swamped him and vied with logic for top billing. He knew what it was. Last night she had told him she hadn't wanted him and it had tripped his ego again. So okay, maybe he should just call the whole wager thing off as he'd thought of doing during his morning swim.

And maybe he would have if someone Eleanore was talking to hadn't made some comment about her shoes—pitch-black stilettos with red soles and a thin red strap that manacled her ankle—because she'd twisted sideways and her calf muscle flexed as she glanced at her feet as if to check what she had put on them. As she did, her suit jacket gaped just enough that he'd been able to see what she had on underneath. Or rather didn't have on.

It was at that point she'd noticed him in the doorway and the warm smile she'd bestowed on his employees had turned into a stunned moue.

The other staff members had noticed him too, and had made moves to take their seats around the table.

Lukas hadn't shifted his eyes off Eleanore though and she'd stiffened under his insatiable regard like a soldier reporting for duty. *Game on*, her body language had said to his, and he'd found himself as hard as an untried youth poring over a girlie magazine.

Not only that but thoughts of her had kept him awake for a long time the night before and he wondered if he had done the same to her.

So he'd held out a chair for her. 'Miss Harrington,' he'd said smoothly, 'I believe this is your seat.' She hadn't wanted to sit beside him—he'd seen that right away—but her professionalism had won out and she'd taken the seat he'd offered with consummate grace. Then she'd set her laptop on the table in front of her and shifted away from him as much as she could.

Now, while he waited for everyone to quieten down, he couldn't help letting her know he knew her secret.

'What I'm talking about, Eleanore,' he

drawled, 'is that I never would have expected you to fight dirty.'

'I do not fight dirty,' she forced out.

'You don't think going braless is fighting dirty? And who would have thought you were the type. I approve by the way.'

'I did not go braless for you!' She looked at him and he almost felt sorry for her when she blushed.

Noticing the avid glances of his employees Lukas introduced her to the group of five and outlined her impressive credentials. Once he was finished he smiled as she completely ignored him and took the floor.

She had clearly prepared herself for the morning and he was impressed with her articulate speech even though she'd once again butchered his language and told the team she was very happy to head up the project and worked to look forward with them. No one had laughed at her gaffe and he supposed that was because she exuded just the right mix of authority and genuine warmth. What shone through was that although she had grown up in a privileged household she worked hard and was clearly passionate about her job. And everyone liked her, he realised, including him.

He liked her very much, especially the inordinate amount of bare skin she had flashed beneath her fitted jacket and flimsy scarf. It made him want to open up her jacket button by button to reveal exactly what she had worn to tempt him with underneath.

She handed out a sheath of papers she must have printed off that morning and Lukas flicked through them quickly. They were ideas for the guest bedrooms and as the others looked through them more slowly she explained her vision.

'We have thirty rooms in total that need to be themed. As our target audience is predominantly couples we want the rooms to look sexy.' She paused to clear her throat and he withheld a smile as one of their earlier conversations replayed in his mind. He liked that he affected her. Very much.

'I've drawn up ideas for ten of the rooms,' she continued. 'And I don't mind that some of the themes are repeated, but we want originality. We also need someone to source the textiles for the individual rooms and public areas.'

Lukas didn't join in the brainstorming session but instead found himself distracted by her scent and the graceful movement of her hands as she spoke. She wore a small gold signet ring on her left-hand pinkie finger and he wondered if an ex-lover had given it to her. Or a current one. The thought had his gut tightening even though he knew he didn't have any claim to her.

When she suddenly stopped talking he realised he'd moved his leg closer to hers and that his knee was pressed firmly against her thigh. Would she move hers away or leave it there?

Eleanore curled her toes inside her shoes when she felt the light pressure of Lukas's knee against her own. She knew what he was doing: making her sit beside him, invading her personal space, looking sexy in another dark suit and open-necked shirt that he knew drew a woman's eye to the masculine column of his tanned neck and the whorl of hair that just peeked out the top and made her wonder how thick it was and how far across his chest it spread.

Knowing she should have been immune to his lady-killer charm didn't stop Eleanore from wondering how it would feel to be held in his arms. How it would feel to make love with him... Which made no sense at all because she'd never had trouble focusing on her goals before. Never even been tempted to deviate from them. Structure was important to her and it was something Isabelle had always admired about her.

'You're so practical, El, it's really impressive. You put your head down and don't let anything get in your way.'

And she wouldn't let Mr Smooth-Talking Kuznetskov get in her way either, Eleanore thought. But how in the world did he know she wasn't wearing a bra? Or that she wasn't the type? She grimaced. She didn't know what upset her the most: that he had guessed that she was braless or that he had guessed she wasn't the type who went braless. She blew out a frustrated breath. Maybe she *should* see a shrink when she returned to the US. Because sleeping with her pseudo-boss—which would no doubt be wonderful a little voice on her shoulder assured her—was definitely not on any of her list of goals.

'Eleanore?'

Embarrassed to be caught mentally drifting she subtly moved her leg away from his and tapped her computer mouse as if she'd been lost in more productive thoughts than what it would be like to sleep with him. 'I'm sorry, I missed that.'

'I asked if you had anything else to say to the team.'

'No. No. Just.' She cleared her throat and addressed the small group. *'Eto zdorovo vstretit'sya s vami bylo.'*

Everyone clapped and one by one left the conference room.

Lukas leant closer to her and repeated her last sentence back to her but in a different order. She frowned. 'What did I say?'

'You said it great meet you was.'

'Oh…I'm terrible at languages.'

He laughed. 'You don't say.'

Her eyes widened. 'You could be nice about it.'

'And then where would we be.'

In bed, Eleanore thought, and had to blink to clear the image from her consciousness.

As the last person filed out of the room she waited for Lukas to do the same. He didn't. He just sat there and watched her with those wicked blue eyes so she gathered her stuff together and pretended she wasn't flustered at the thought that he would mention her underwear again.

'Did you sleep well last night?' he asked, his pleasant tone winding her nerves even tighter.

'Fine, thanks. And you?'

'Not so much.' He took a sip from his water glass. 'I dreamt about getting you naked.'

Eleanore twisted her mother's ring on her little finger. 'I know what you're trying to do,' she said crisply, 'and it won't work.'

He leaned back in his chair. 'It won't?'

'No.' It occurred to her that she really should be trying to tempt him and she briefly considered slipping off her scarf on the pretext of being hot but at the last minute she chickened out. The only real experience she had with flirting was watching actresses in movies and they never fluffed their lines.

'Going somewhere?' he drawled.

Eleanore held her files and computer to her chest. 'Work.'

Of course he chuckled, the husky sound following her down the hallway.

By the end of the week Eleanore found herself jumping at shadows and she was no longer dressing to tempt him. It was too stressful and he was a much better player than her.

While she spent her time trying to avoid him he called her into his office on the smallest pretext or stopped by hers to go over things with her. And she had no choice but to put up with it.

On one of the days he'd even taken lunch in her office. Or rather, dessert. It had been one of the office girls' birthday and he'd brought cake. Chocolate cake. Only one slice and one fork.

'Want some?' There was a dangerous gleam

in his eyes and his smile widened as she pressed herself back against her chair.

'No.'

He perched on the end of her desk. 'On a diet?'

Eleanore ignored the heat rising to her cheeks. 'That's hardly polite.'

'You don't need to diet. You're tiny.' His mocking gaze lingered on her chest. 'Well, most of you is tiny.' Ignoring her sharp inhalation at his rudeness he tilted the plate in her direction. 'It's good.'

She didn't need him to tell her that. She knew it would be good. She could smell it from across her desk. Saw the way he tipped the fork over in his mouth and used his tongue to suck all the chocolate away. 'You don't know what you're missing out on.'

Oh, she was pretty sure that she did.

His smirk as he swirled his tongue around the fork infuriated her and his lazy smile told her he knew it.

'I'm busy.'

'Anything I can do for you?'

'Find a main road and go play on it,' she suggested sweetly.

He chuckled. 'How about you kiss me instead and put us both out of our misery.'

'Who said I was miserable?'

Tired. Grumpy. Wound up tighter than one of her father's old fishing reels. Yes. And okay, maybe a teensy bit miserable.

Spying the next forkful of decadent cake he was about to put in his mouth the little devil on Eleanore's shoulder made her reach out and snag his wrist.

He went predator still at her actions, curiosity lighting the depths of his blue eyes and Eleanore cursed her impulsiveness. She'd intended the move to be brief. She'd wanted to turn the tables and show him that two could play at this silly game of seduction. Only the skin beneath her fingers was warm and dry, the hair on his wrist slightly rough against her palm and her awareness of him skyrocketed. Her heart beat wildly inside her chest and it was sheer pride that had her redirecting the fork to her own mouth and away from his.

Knowing it was too late to back down she ignored the rush of colour that stung her cheekbones and closed her eyes as she quickly drew the cake into her mouth. 'Mmmm.' She slowly eased back in her chair as if she was completely unaffected by what she'd done and forced herself to keep looking at him as his gaze raked over her face and settled on her mouth.

The cake turned to glue but she pretended

it was ambrosia as she swallowed. 'You were right, it is good.'

She noticed that the blue of his eyes was almost entirely eaten up by his pupils and she was just congratulating herself for getting one up on him when he reached across the expanse of the desk and placed his thumb against the corner of her mouth.

Her breath stuttered and then stopped as the rough pad of his thumb traced a gentle path across her lower lip. Instant weakness pervaded her limbs and she felt light headed as arousal coursed through her and settled in an ache between her thighs.

'A crumb,' he murmured, his voice so low it was almost inaudible. 'Do you want it?'

Completely mesmerized by the dark sweep of his lashes as he watched her, Eleanore did something she'd never even had the remotest urge to do before. She opened her mouth and drew his thumb inside.

His taste exploded against her tongue, dark and earthy. Slightly musky with just a hint of the sweet chocolate. But it was him that she tasted. Him that made her heart race. Instinct seemed to take over and she wound her tongue around his thumb and sucked lightly.

She wasn't sure which one of them made a low noise but the sound made her jerk back, releasing his now moist flesh. She lifted heavy eyes to his and absently noted the dull colour highlighting his cheekbones and the way his eyes glittered dangerously down into hers. For a minute she thought he was going to devour her, the look of hunger was so stark on his taut features. Fortunately someone knocked on her door and the tension in the air broke like a line of cotton held too tight for too long.

Lukas mumbled something under his breath in his own language and fired her a dark look. 'Until next time, *moya krasavitsa.*'

Feeling like a puppet who had just been set aside Eleanore would have gladly slumped in her chair if not for the girl who had just entered her office.

Smiling brightly she tried once again to put Lukas Kuznetskov out of her mind, knowing that with every maddening interaction they had it became harder and harder to do.

That night she dreamt of him licking chocolate sauce off her body. When she woke up she was sweaty and uncomfortable and her mood didn't improve when she realised that all her work shirts were dirty because she'd been so exhausted from long hours working each day she hadn't gone down to the communal laundry or located a dry-cleaning service. Spying the new sleeveless blouse she'd impulsively purchased two days ago from a nearby boutique she wondered if she'd dare wear it to the office. She didn't know what had possessed her to buy it. It wasn't her typical style—a little low cut in the front and made from the sheerest cream silk she'd ever touched—but at least she could wear a bra with it, and if she kept her jacket on...

Remembering that Lukas would be out of town all day looking at his ships or something, she didn't waste time searching for anything else but combined it with a smart Chanel-style skirt suit with a cropped jacket. She added her favourite black boots and tied her hair back in a sleek ponytail.

Feeling more like her normal self she was almost whistling by the time she reached her office and shoved Lukas firmly out of her mind as she got down to it.

'Good to see you've put underwear on today.'

Eleanore turned sharply to find Lukas loitering in her doorway. She slammed the filing cabinet in her office closed and marched over to her desk. She grabbed the jacket from the back of her chair and stuffed her arms into it.

'Please, don't cover up on my account.'

'What do you want?'

His eyebrows slowly climbed his forehead. 'Grumpy this morning?'

Only because she'd felt her heart leap into her throat when she'd heard his voice and now it was knocking around behind her ribs as if it was looking for a way out.

The dream she'd had appeared front and centre in her mind. As did the taste of his skin on her mouth.

He strolled into her office and closed the door, the pale blue shirt he wore making the striking blue of his eyes stand out in his gorgeous Viking face. 'Why, Eleanore, you don't seem to be in a very good mood this morning.'

'I'm fine. Just busy.' Ignoring her he perched on the corner of her desk as if he had nothing better to do in the whole world.

'On your hotel,' she added pointedly, pretending rapt attention in her computer screen.

She should have known he wouldn't take the hint and leave. Instead he reached across her desk and confiscated her orange notebook. It was the one she wrote her goals in and she'd felt the need to go over them before starting work that morning.

'Give me that—it's private.'

'"Long-Range Goals."' His eyes sparkled mischievously. '"1. Promotion. 2. Investment property. 3. Own business? 4. Marriage. 5. Family."'

'Don't you have any conscience at all?'

'You already know I don't. I take it *family* refers to some future event and not your siblings.'

'Give it back.'

'I must say I'm surprised to see marriage way down on your list. It's usually on the top for most of the women I date.'

'Just another reason why we'll never date.'

'That only makes me want to date you even more. You have your head screwed on straight.'

'Just knowing you're one of those lame commitment-phobes warms my heart,' she mocked.

He smiled. 'What's the promotion?'

'I'm not discussing this with you.'

Ignoring her outstretched hand he regarded her levelly. 'Do you actually stick to this?'

'No, I have it for fun.'

He glanced at the list again, shook his head. '*Nyet*. "Fun" isn't on here.'

Eleanore kept her hand out with the exaggerated patience of a parent at the end of her tether.

'And why the question mark after "own business"?'

'Will you please give that back?'

She waited for him to make another comment but instead he just smiled, handed her the notebook and pulled his phone from his pocket, scrolling through his messages and winding her nerves even tighter.

Last night she'd nearly sent the wrong plans to the wrong recipients because her mind had been on him instead of her job and, after yesterday's little thumb-sucking episode, she knew she was too tense to continue with more of his games this morning. And while she'd never thought of herself as a quitter, right now she was ready to wave the white flag which just made her temper spike. 'Are you going to sit here all day?'

His eyes shifted from his phone to hers. 'Is that an invitation, Miss Harrington?' he asked softly.

Realising he was a master strategist and she'd been dancing to his tune all week Eleanore jumped out of her chair. If he wanted her office, he could have it. She needed to visit the site to check on progress anyway. She'd just do that now and leave her paperwork for later.

Of course she should have known that he wouldn't let her leave without asking where she was going but she hadn't expected for him to reach out and snag hold of her wrist on her way past.

'Going somewhere?'

'To the site.' Her voice sounded scratchy and she cleared it. 'If you want my office it's all yours.'

'But I don't want your office.'

His deliberately low tone followed by a sensuous smirk told her that he wanted her instead and a terrible weakness invaded her limbs.

'I can't do this any more,' she said on a rush.

His grip around her wrist was dry and warm. 'Can't do what?' His thumb stroked across the pulse point going mad beneath her skin and a shiver raced down her spine.

'This.'

'This?'

Was he being deliberately obtuse?

'Us.' She tugged on her wrist but instead of giving her freedom he urged her closer.

'Us?'

Eleanore moistened her lips with the tip of her tongue and realised that hadn't been the best move when Lukas tracked the movement, his eyes much darker when they returned to hers and without a trace of humour in them. She saw a muscle tick in his jaw and her breathing became laboured as she realised he'd manoeuvred her between his open thighs.

A thrill of anticipation shot through her. Anticipation entwined with fear and while she could have moved away—he wasn't holding her that tightly—she felt like she was staring into the eyes of a cobra about to strike. Only this one wasn't about to inflict pain but abject pleasure.

'You know what I'm talking about,' she breathed. 'This silly bet thing. It's highly inappropriate.'

'Highly.' His hungry gaze slide down her torso and his hands moved to lightly grip her hips, each one of his fingers spreading either side of her spine in the small of her back.

Oh, dear Lord.

She could feel the warmth of those big palms and her insides flooded with liquid heat and her nipples hardened to achy points. Her mind suddenly filled with a vision of him sliding his hands lower to gather the hem of her skirt before pushing the constricting fabric upward until his fingers could trace around the edge of her underwear before slipping inside.

Eleanore bit into her bottom lip to stifle a groan.

Never before had she had such X-rated thoughts about a man and her hands fluttered awkwardly between them as part of her wanted to place them on his wide shoulders for support and another part warned her that she might lose more than Harrington's name on the door if she did. She might lose her heart as well.

Normally she thought of herself as assertive and practical—a card-carrying feminist, as he'd called her—but right now she had no idea where her willpower had gone. And it was all his fault. Telling her he wouldn't kiss her, talking about her bra, eating chocolate cake in her office, watching her with those beautiful blue eyes...

'Why don't you kiss me, *moya Eleanore*, and end it.'

Some small stash of sanity inside her brain asserted itself and she shook her head. He brought his mouth closer to hers and she stupidly feared that he would stop and continue at the same time. He was like the devil tempting her over to the dark side.

His strong fingers massaged her hip bones and she grabbed hold of his wide shoulders for support. His hard muscles bunched powerfully beneath her touch, tension coming off his long, lean body in seismic waves.

A small sound escaped her closed lips and he swore, dragging her still closer until barely an inch separated them. 'Then I will.' Before she could comprehend his intention one big palm lifted to the nape of her neck and dragged her mouth to his.

It felt like he had dangled this particular carrot in front of her for so long that when his lips slid over hers in a feather-light touch, nibbling and pulling at her sensitive skin Eleanore didn't even think of resisting.

Instead she kissed him back with a hunger she wouldn't have thought possible, her lips opening beneath the erotic pressure of his until his tongue swept into her mouth and drugged her senses.

Eleanore whimpered low in her throat and wrapped her arms around his neck as her legs buckled beneath her weight. A tiny warning bell rang somewhere in the deep recesses of her psyche but that was about the time he pushed her jacket wide and swept his hands from her face to her hips and skimmed the outer swells of her breasts. A frustrated kind of pleasure ripped through her and made her arch toward him until her breasts flattened against his chest.

He must have liked the move because he growled against her neck and reversed their positions so that the edge of her desk bit into her bottom and it was his turn to stand between her open thighs. He lifted her onto it and then palmed her full breasts, his thumbs going straight to her rigid nipples to strum over their achy points.

Eleanore squirmed to get closer to him as pleasure knifed through her and damp heat flooded her lower body. He must have liked that too, because she felt the cooler air on her inner thighs as her skirt was hiked higher and her stomach muscles clenched when Lukas bent his knees a little to press even closer.

Something sharp dug into her bottom as his movements became more urgent and less co-ordinated and she jerked in his arms.

'Easy, *moya krasavitsa*,' he crooned, his fingers working impatiently at the hidden hook-and-eye fastenings of her top.

The sound of his voice was enough to break into Eleanore's reverie long enough for her to realise what she was doing. And who she was doing it with.

'What are you doing?'

Lukas raised his head and she saw a line of hot colour darkening the tips of his Slavic cheekbones. 'What? I am being too rough?' His normally fluent English was nowhere in evidence. 'Come, let me kiss you. *Vash rot tak sladko*. Your mouth is so sweet.'

He lowered his head and claimed her lips again in a powerful kiss that drove every pellet of common sense from her mind and sent all her attention to the hollow, achy space between her thighs.

Trying to assuage it she closed her legs around his hard hips but that only heightened the sensation of emptiness.

Appalled at her uncontrolled reaction she clamped down on the sensation and pulled her mouth from his. 'No—Lukas—stop.' She arched away from him. 'We can't do this. My office…the door…Lukas!' She shoved at his shoulders and knew she'd gotten through to him when he went dead still.

'You kissed me,' she gasped, suddenly remembering their bet.

'Yes.' His breathing was as laboured as hers. 'I seem to have no control where you are concerned.'

His head descended toward hers but she pulled back before his lips could claim hers again. 'What about the bet?'

When he looked at her his eyes were hooded. 'You win. Congratulations.'

Eleanore frowned. 'I win?'

'And I lose. Now kiss me again. I need to taste you on my tongue.'

'No.' Her addled brain was trying to tell her something and then she got it and stilled. 'You don't care.'

'On the contrary, I care very much.'

'No. I mean about the bet.'

'Oh, that.' He shrugged and dragged a hand through his hair. 'That not so much.'

'But how can you not?'

His dark gaze held hers. 'The hotel is still mine. I don't need to have my name on it to know that. Attachments will always make you weak.'

She slipped off the desk and out of his arms, her mind reeling. 'I can't believe this.'

He stared at her as she put distance between them, his smile pure sex. 'I can't believe I waited a week to kiss you. You're like a firecracker in my arms.'

She shook her head. 'Don't you have any morals?'

'None.'

His face had become a hard, impassive mask, hiding his thoughts from her. Instinct told her not to believe him. But what kind of person made a bet they didn't care about?

The type who didn't care about anything at all, a rational voice informed her.

And she'd always known he was like that. Right from the start. So why was she prevaricating? Did she want him to be more than he said he was?

Closing her eyes, her body still humming from where he had touched her, she hardened her resolve. 'I don't want you to touch me again.'

'You liked it a minute ago.'

'Well, I don't like it now.' She gulped air into her lungs like a dying goldfish. 'You're not my type and… and apart from that it's completely unprofessional. I'm here to work on your hotel. As soon as it's completed I'm leaving.'

His gaze dropped to her lips. Eleanore could almost feel the warmth of his mouth as if he was still kissing her. She tried to blink the effect away but when her eyes lifted to his once more his held a mocking light as if he could see right through her flimsy denial. His next words confirmed as much.

'Keep telling yourself that and you might even believe it.'

CHAPTER SEVEN

HE WASN'T HER TYPE. The irritation that had sparked in him at those words still hadn't waned. At the time Lukas had determined to forget all about the attraction he felt for her. All week he'd taken meetings out of the office and kept away from her but still he noticed her presence. Or more, *felt* her presence. Just as he also felt her absence. Like now. He didn't need to go to her office to know it would be empty. It was the oddest sensation and one he couldn't explain.

Nor could he explain how he'd nearly lost control with her last week. If she hadn't stopped him he'd have taken her right there on her desk with the door unlocked and damn the consequences.

Frustration gnawed at his gut. He couldn't stop thinking about her. Or the way she made him feel. Somehow alive and more engaged in life than he had been in a long time. And she wanted him. Not that she would admit it.

Another bite of frustration clenched his stomach. Should he apologise to her for letting things get out of hand in her office last week? And would it make any difference? And what would he say? *Can we start over? Invite her to dinner?* No point in that. It wasn't as if he was desperate. He could call up any number of women from here to Australia and have a beautiful woman in his bed moments later. Well, maybe hours later if she was from Australia, but dammit, where was she?

'Where's who?'

Lukas hadn't heard Petra come up behind him and he scowled at her. 'No one.'

'Are you muttering about Eleanore?'

His PA had been regarding him strangely all week. The last thing he needed to do was set off her romantic radar over his conflicted emotions about Eleanore. She already gave him enough grief over his choice of women. 'I don't mutter,' he said. 'But where is she?'

The lift pinged behind him and his blood fired in his veins. Only it wasn't Eleanore, it was Zoe, the staff member who had admired Eleanore's shoes in the conference room.

'Good afternoon, Petra. Mr Kuznetskov.' She blushed prettily. 'Eleanore said to leave these on your desk.'

'Is she at the hotel?'

Zoe's eyes widened and he told himself to tone it down. 'No, Greg and some of the guys took her to a couple of bars,' she informed him enthusiastically. Then she offered him the drawings in her hand. 'You should see these. They're the images Eleanore created of the arched walkway that links the hotel with the group of individual chalets the guests use as warm rooms. It makes the whole design interconnected like a smaller snowflake clinging to a larger one. It seems like an obvious thing to do in hindsight, but I never would have thought of it.'

Lukas frowned. They said a man's IQ halved when he thought with his penis. His, it seemed, fell even more. 'Bars? Which bars?'

'Good to see you've got time to relax at a bar when there is only two weeks left until opening night.'

Just about to knock the number ten billiard ball into the upper right-hand pocket Eleanore straightened and flung her head around so sharply at the sound of Lukas's voice the ends of her smooth ponytail whipped around and slapped her in the face. 'Lukas!'

She glanced at him warily. She hadn't seen him all week, not since he'd kissed her in his office, and she still hadn't reconciled the woman who had fallen into his arms like a ripe melon with the woman she thought herself to be. Someone who was independent and ambitious and just a little afraid of what would happen if she fell for a man and he didn't fall for her right back.

Not that she'd fallen for Lukas Kuznetskov or anything. She was far too sensible for that but still… She was annoyed when during the week she had caught herself listening for the sound of his footsteps in the hallway and periodically glancing at her doorway only to find that no, he wasn't loitering there watching her.

'*Privet*, Lukas.' Greg came around the table to greet him, keeping a respectful distance between them as if acknowledging that Lukas was the alpha in the room.

Greg said something to him in Russian and Eleanore knew it was about her because Lukas's eyes narrowed in on her.

'It seems you're a pool shark, Miss Harrington.'

'The things you learn at university,' she said, attempting lightness.

'How to play truant being one of them.' It wasn't a friendly comment and Eleanore frowned.

His earlier words about relaxing came back to her and her good mood faded. Apart from her insidious attraction for him she thought everything was going okay.

'I'm not slacking off,' she said, annoyed that she felt the need to defend herself. 'This is work.'

'Bar hopping and playing pool is work?' His eyebrows rose in mock surprise. 'You have a better job than I do.'

She noticed Mikhail, the sculptor, and Dominic, the electrician, had also come around the table and were listening. 'Mikhail is going to sculpt a billiard table to go into the smaller second bar and Dominic has been showing me different lighting options. So yes, we're working.'

'Really?' His mouth curled with derision as he took in the row of empty shot glasses lining the shelf along the wall. 'From what I can see it looks more like you're working on improving your drinking capacity.'

The heavy silence that fell over their small group was palpable.

'Yes.' Eleanore smiled, furious that he should question her like this in front of the others. She'd worked hard to gain the respect of these hard-living workmen who were unused to dealing with a woman on-site and to have Lukas come across all patriarchal made her blood boil. 'And I do believe it was your suggestion that Russia was the best place for me to earn my stripes,' she reminded him with enough sugar to fell a wedding cake.

The men threw her a curious glance because they all knew she hadn't touched one of the vodka shots they had ordered. 'Besides,' she added quickly before one of them took it upon himself to correct her, 'I wasn't aware that I had to account for my time twenty-four hours a day.'

'You do if it impacts the opening of my ice hotel,' he said grimly.

Right now she wanted to tell him to shove his ice hotel. 'Lucky this doesn't.'

She noticed a muscle work in his jaw and was pleased she had irritated him because he was certainly irritating her!

'Tell me,' he grated silkily, 'was your sister pleased to find out that Harrington's name will be on the front of the hotel?'

Eleanore angled her chin up. 'As a matter of fact she was.'

'And did you also tell her how you got it there?'

'Oh!' Unable to hide her shocked gasp, hot colour streaked across her cheekbones.

Greg glanced warily between the two of them and said something to Lukas in a placating tone and it made her feel even more like a fool. 'Mr Kuznetskov?' she interrupted Greg. 'Is there something you wanted because otherwise we'd like to continue our meeting?'

'I want an update on my hotel.'

'I should be free tomorrow morning.'

'Now.'

'Sorry. I'm busy now.'

Lukas turned toward the men and spoke to them in Russian. Incensed Eleanore grabbed his forearm and felt the corded muscles tense beneath her fingertips. 'What did you just say to them?'

His eyes drilled into hers like ice blue chips. 'I just told them this meeting is over.'

'How dare you!' she rasped under her breath.

'It is okay, Eleanore.' Dominic pulled his wallet from his pocket and pulled out a few *ruble*. 'I think I know what it is that you want with the lighting. How about we meet tomorrow afternoon at the hotel and I will show you what I propose.'

Lukas told Dominic that he would pick up the tab and Eleanore didn't care that it was a nice gesture. Banking her anger she thanked the men and waved them off, leaving her and Lukas alone in the noisy bar.

Lukas pushed his jacket open as he shoved his hands on his hips, leaning toward her. 'I went to three bars before I found you here.'

'What do you want?' Eleanore fumed. 'A medal or a chest to pin it on?'

They glared at each other. 'I want you to focus on my hotel and not the men working on it.'

'I can see why your last architect quit,' she fumed, absolute fury making her insides quake. 'You're a control freak.'

She made to push past him but he laid his hand on her shoulder. 'Where are you going?'

'*Do not* touch me. And *do not* question me. I'm off the clock right now.' She pointed her finger at him. 'How dare you come in here and treat me like some wayward child and undermine my authority. This was a business meeting between me and my site managers and you completely undermined my authority.'

'At the slightest encouragement either one of those men would have shown you more than lighting options and sculpting ideas.'

'What?' Disbelief coursed through her. 'I can't believe you just said that!' she seethed.

Lukas couldn't believe he'd just said it either. It was as if the vision of Eleanore leaning over the pool table in her tight skirt and those black stilettos with the red ankle straps had fried his brain. But more than that it drove him crazy just thinking about her with someone else.

'You're nothing but a sexist chauvinist who has the hormonal intelligence of a teenage boy. Or not even.' She looked like she was getting ready to punch him. 'That's an insult to teenage boys!'

'And you're a pampered princess too used to people bowing and scraping to your every need.' It wasn't true and Lukas knew it even as he said it. She worked far too hard and cared far too much about the job to be the princess type. Still, he wasn't a sexist chauvinist either although he would agree that right now he had the emotional intelligence of a teenage boy.

'Me!'

She threw him a filthy look and he just wanted to kiss the snarl from her lips.

'If anyone here is used to people bowing and scraping it's you. Splashing your money around, making rude comments when it suits you, *threatening* people.'

'Threatening people? Who have I threatened?'

'Me! When you told me you'd go to the Chatsfields if I didn't agree to work for you.'

He laughed. What else could he do? 'If you're so paranoid about the Chatsfields that's your problem, and as for you working for me, I think you love it.'

She stepped closer to him and he caught a

whiff of apples. *O Bozhe*, but he loved apples. 'I think you're deluded so...'

Later Lukas would tell himself he wasn't the type to grab a woman in a public bar even if they were near a darkened corner—later when he was asking himself a lot of questions. Right now he was fed up with her mouthiness. Fed up with the overpowering need to touch her that had driven him to behave like a fool in front of his men and so he did what he'd wanted to do again all week. He bent his head and captured her mouth with his own.

As soon as his lips touched hers reality receded and took every one of his brain cells with it. Especially when instead of pushing him away as he expected her to do she curled her small hands into the front of his jacket and pulled him in even closer.

She kissed him back as if she'd been dreaming of him as much as he had of her and all his reasons for staying away from her just dissolved in a puddle of need. He widened her mouth with his and thrust his tongue deep, mating with hers—all his frustration and irritation and anger of the past week pouring out of him and into that kiss.

Only half aware that they were in a crowded bar, Lukas pushed his hands beneath the hem of her red shirt and caressed the silky skin of her waist. She was soft and pliant and she just seemed to melt into him, her breasts thrusting toward his chest and grazing the hard wall of his abdomen. Growling deep in his throat Lukas slid one hand around to her butt and cupped her, raising her onto her toes so he could settle the weight of his aching erection between the cradle of her thighs.

She let out a breathy little moan and the sound was like the time he'd thrown gunpowder on a bin fire and nearly burnt himself alive. He just went up in flames and his greedy mouth slid down the slender column of her neck and lapped at her honeyed skin.

'Poluchit' nomer!' A gruff voice called from behind him, laughing.

Get a room?

Bozhe!

Pulling back Lukas waited for Eleanore's glazed eyes to open before he let her go. He needed to adjust the front of his pants but fortunately the lighting of the bar was low enough that he hoped he got away without doing so. 'I'm going to pick up your tab. Wait here.'

Dazed, Eleanore stared after Lukas's broad back as he wound his way through the crowd of people. She touched her tongue to her kiss-swollen lips and glanced around. A few men near the pool table gave her suggestive looks and she wanted to die of embarrassment. How had she gone from anger to passion in the space of seconds?

And what was she doing waiting here like a good girl for Lukas to come back and get her? The man had just proven that he was the egotistical arrogant jackass that she knew him to be. And she wouldn't kiss him again if her life depended on it!

Furious with herself and with him and completely unnerved by the strength of her response to him, not to mention the tingling sensation that remained from where he'd pressed his so-large-it-had-to-be-fake erection between her thighs, she didn't wait to see where he was but rushed out of the bar.

It was dark even though it must have been barely six o'clock and a blast of cold air bit into her face and scythed the thoughts from her head.

Digging into her pocket for her gloves and hat she realised that she had left the beautiful coat Lukas had chosen for her back on the shelf near the pool table. Not that she cared. So what if he'd chosen something she loved. Arrogant ass. She didn't need it anyway. Much.

She peered down the street in search of a cab but saw only a stream of evening traffic and a bunch of pedestrians hurrying in and out of shops. Remembering that they had visited this particular bar last because it was close to her apartment building she took a second to get her bearings. Then she saw a shoe store she had been meaning to investigate and knew which direction she needed to go and headed along the snow-covered pavement toward the sanctuary of her apartment.

She only wished she'd remembered to change into sensible boots before leaving the office earlier. After the sultry heat of Singapore it was fair to say she still hadn't adjusted to the wintery conditions in St Petersburg.

Five minutes, she decided, and she'd be home and she'd thaw out under a hot shower. That decided she tucked her chin into her suit jacket and quickened her pace.

Within a block she realised she'd turned the wrong way down a quieter street and pivoted on her heel to backtrack only to hear the faint mewling of a young child down an alleyway. Or was it an animal?

Immediately wary of the darkness she peered into the alley and saw a small kitten not too far down clawing at the snow as if it was trapped between two garbage cans. 'Oh, you poor darling. It's okay.' She didn't even think twice before she approached the pathetic little thing and crouched down so as not to scare it. She saw immediately that one of its back legs was wrapped in string.

It was so tiny and it was shivering with cold, its fur all matted and wet. Reaching forward she gripped the scruff of its neck so that it didn't bite her and tugged on the string. It came away easily in her hand and she only realised why when a dark shape rose up from behind the garbage cans and reached out for her. Instinctively Eleanore grabbed the kitten close and fell backward onto the dirty snow, screaming as the plastic garbage can fell on top of her, spewing out its contents.

Struggling to sit up she just made out the dirty face of a young kid as he leapt over the garbage and grabbed her arm. Thinking he was about to hit her Eleanore screamed again and raised her free hand and realised that he was pulling at the straps of her handbag. Suddenly there was the sound of heavy footsteps running toward them and with one almighty yank that nearly ripped her shoulder from its socket her assailant was off her. She heard him scrambling beside her in the snow and then he took off around a narrow opening between the buildings.

Not waiting to see if the person who had come to her aid was a friend or a foe, Eleanore clutched the petrified kitten that was scratching at her jacket and rolled to a crouched position as all the self-defence instructions she'd learned a couple of years ago—but had never had reason to use—came flooding back.

A male swore above her as he pulled her to her feet and Eleanore sagged with relief. 'Lukas! Oh, my God. You scared the life out of me.'

'*I* did!' he roared. 'What the hell do you think you're doing?'

She remembered her anger at him from the bar and it warred with her fear. 'Walking home.'

'Down an alley!'

'No. There was a kitten…' Saying it out loud sounded dumb even to her own ears but Eleanore had never been able to walk past an injured animal or a crying child without stopping. She remembered all too well what it was like to feel alone in the world and she wouldn't wish it on her worst enemy. Feeling the kitten tremble against her she eased her grip on the poor thing and cuddled it against her jacket to reassure it.

'Let me guess,' Lukas spat. 'It was tied to the bin.'

Eleanore's eyes widened. 'Has it happened to you as well?'

'No.' He reached down to pick up a dark shape from the ground. 'I've done it before.'

'What?'

The dark shape turned out to be her beloved overcoat and he wasn't gentle as he bundled it around her shoulders. 'Of all the gullible, idiotic things to do...' He shook his head. 'I told you earlier that St Petersburg wasn't the wonderland you think it is and why in hell didn't you wait for me to take you home?'

'Because I don't want you to take me home.' But now that she'd had time to process what had actually happened her anger toward him wasn't quite as strong as it had been back at the bar. 'Thank you for helping me,' she said stiffly.

His face was all harsh angles and shadows as he glared down at her in the dim light. 'Don't thank me. I'm too angry. You could have ended up dead. Are you hurt?' he added gruffly.

'No. Thankfully he was only a kid. At least I think he was a kid.'

'They can be worse than the adults,' Lukas said grimly. 'More desperate and much more unpredictable. Come, my car is waiting at the kerb. Can you walk?'

'Of course.' Relief that he'd come after her made her feel weak and for once she didn't argue.

He held the back door of the Mercedes open for her. 'Get in.'

She cradled the kitten inside her overcoat as she did as he asked.

Lukas followed her into the car and glowered at the lump on her chest from the opposite seat. 'What are you planning to do with that thing?'

'She's not a thing and I can't leave her in the snow. She'll die.'

'Survival of the fittest, Eleanore, it's what makes the world go round.'

'That's not true.'

The look he gave her said he thought she was an idiot. And maybe she was. She was certainly a lucky one even though she was pretty sure she would have been all right if the kid had managed to take her bag but she was also glad she didn't have to test the theory.

'Will I have to file a police report?'

Lukas turned his brooding expression back from the window. 'There are over sixteen thousand street kids in St Petersburg and you just fell for one of the oldest tricks on the streets so there's not much point.'

'Sixteen thousand!' She frowned. 'How do you know how many street kids there are in the city?' She would have no idea if asked the same question in New York.

The Mercedes pulled up outside her apartment building and Lukas helped her out while his driver held the door, his breath fogging in front of his face.

Eleanore's legs didn't seem to want to work properly and he must have read her mind because he firmed his grip beneath her elbow. She wondered if he'd make some reference to feminists or her brainlessness but he remained big and silent beside her until they reached her door.

'Keys.'

'Lukas, really…'

'If you know what's good for you you'll stop arguing with me and give me the keys.'

Exasperated by his harsh tone and grudgingly glad of his help at the same time Eleanore handed over her handbag. How she found someone so bossy and so controlling so utterly attractive was beyond rational thought. It just went to show that you couldn't trust hormones.

'You might want to go and change.'

Eleanore looked down and realised that her skirt and stockings were caked with mud from the melted snow and dirt and that she smelt like garbage. 'I have to take care of the kitten.'

He pulled a disgusted face. 'Give it to me.'

'What are you going to do with her?'

He lifted the spitting, mewling creature from her arms and it looked tiny as he brought it up to his wide chest. 'Not much. It's too small to turn into a hat.'

'A hat! You wouldn't…' She stopped. Looked at him. 'You're teasing me,' she realised with a start.

'I'm going to put it in the utility room.' His gaze raked over her. 'You're shaking. Are you sure you're not hurt?'

'No.' But she felt cold. All over. 'I don't want to put you to any trouble.'

'Too late for that.' He waved her away. 'Go take a shower. I'll take care of this flea bag you insist on keeping.'

Half an hour later and dressed in leggings and an oversize sweatshirt she came back to find Lukas wiping up water on the black-and-white tiles on the kitchen floor. Almost immediately she realised it wasn't water he was cleaning up. 'Was that the kitten?'

He glanced up at her. 'It certainly wasn't me.'

A grin split her face at his pretended chagrin and she stifled a laugh. 'I'm sorry. I could have taken care of that.'

He dumped the soggy paper towels in the trash and washed his hands in the sink. 'I've cleaned up worse.'

A fleeting moment of utter bleakness clouded

his face and she immediately wanted to know what had put it there. Somehow she didn't think it was her, although perhaps she had made it worse… 'You're still angry with me,' she said.

'Absolutely.'

She sighed. 'I don't regret it but what if I admit that what I did was stupid?'

'That's just agreeing with me. Kids on the street are desperate. They'll do anything for money.'

'Anything?'

'*Da*, anything.'

The look in his eyes was hard and edgy and she remembered his comment in the alleyway about the trick she'd fallen for. *'No, I've done it before.'*

Had he spent his childhood on the streets? The idea seemed ludicrous given how well-spoken he was, how cultured, but it would explain that air of danger all the well-made suits in the world couldn't eradicate and it would also explain why there was very little information on him prior to when he was twenty-five and had burst onto the international scene with a rusty fleet of container ships he'd turned into a multimillion-dollar concern by the time he was thirty. Now he seemed to have his hand in everything from ships to shoeshine products and whatever he touched turned to gold.

'Were you a street kid?'

Probably if she'd thought before she'd spoken she wouldn't have blurted the question out like that because he stiffened and that untameable quality that made her blood quicken crossed his face.

For a minute he hesitated and she thought that he was going to confirm her suspicions, that he was going to open up to her, and it surprised her how much she wanted him to do so. How much she cared.

'Nobody could question your imagination, that's for sure, Miss Harrington.' He gave a short laugh as if her idea was ludicrous and Eleanore was embarrassed she'd said anything.

'You won't be able to keep the kitten, you realise,' he added. 'It's probably got fleas. And worse.'

Surprised to find that she'd forgotten all about the kitten Eleanore glanced around the floor guiltily. 'I'm not letting her go. She'll die and I don't care what you say about the survival of the fittest. I'm fit and I'll take care of her. Where is she?'

'*He* is in the laundry.'

'Oh.' She smiled at the slip and for Lukas

it was like the sun coming out from behind a black cloud. Completely dazzling. 'My mistake.'

She headed for the utility room and glanced down at the makeshift essentials he'd provided. 'Um, Lukas, she—I mean, he needs somewhere to go.'

'Go?'

'To the toilet.'

His mouth twisted. 'It seems pretty happy with the floor.'

She laughed and he found himself wanting to grin. Amazing considering how churned up he still felt after nearly spilling his guts to her about his childhood like some old woman in need of comfort. 'A box and some paper should do it. If we have any.'

Needing something to do he opened one of the overhead cupboards and pulled out a couple of older newspapers while Eleanore emptied some vegetables out of a box in the pantry. She cut it down to size and started shredding paper. 'That should do for now.'

She set it down near the kitten, who was currently hiding beneath the bath towel he'd placed on the floor. It hissed like a mutant snake.

'Friendly little thing,' Lukas observed.

'He's been hurt,' she admonished, 'and terrified. Give him time.'

Her soft words made a lump form in his throat because he knew that some wounds could never be healed. Oblivious as she was to such things he watched as she bent toward the kitten and tried to coax it out of hiding. Her patience and gentleness shook something loose inside of him and he swallowed heavily to staunch the flow of emotion he could feel welling up inside of him.

After making a couple of attempts to gain the animal's trust Eleanore decided to leave him alone with the saucer of milk Lukas had provided but which the kitten had yet to touch. She glanced at the man who had shown such gruff tenderness when dealing with the kitten. For some reason she hadn't expected it of him and it threw her.

She couldn't deny that she was curious about him. He was such an enigma; on the one hand seeming to be completely self-centred and uncaring about his impact on others, and on the other someone prepared to construct a hotel for charity and take the time to put a saucer of milk down for a petrified kitten. Someone who tried to make life easier for his employees and who thought about the environment when he'd constructed his office building. Someone she was starting to think she had gravely misjudged.

But maybe that was hormones talking. Because he was also the most attractive man she had ever met and he set her blood on fire just looking at her. Especially when he looked at her in *that* way: as if he wanted her more than any other woman in the world.

She stopped in the living room and felt suddenly awkward when she turned to face him. 'You know, I did look into the alleyway before I ventured down there,' she said, feeling the need to defend herself.

Lukas arched a mocking brow. 'And of course when your attacker didn't announce himself with a warning placard like they obviously do in New York you just thought you'd head on down.'

'No. I heard the kitten crying and I was worried about it. Plus, I know self-defence so I thought I'd be fine.' And weirdly she'd never once felt unsafe in New York. In fact, living in New York had obviously given her a false sense of security because she'd never been confronted with a situation like she had been tonight.

'Show me,' he said thickly.

Startled by the request Eleanore looked up to find his eyelids at half-mast. Her heartbeat galloped as her body responded to the unspoken command from his.

'Show you what?'

'Show me those self-defence skills that obviously made you feel ten feet tall.'

CHAPTER EIGHT

ELEANORE COULDN'T DO THAT. If she did…if she touched him she knew her resolve to maintain a level of professionalism between them would go up in smoke. 'I can't.'

A dangerous gleam had entered his eyes. 'Why not?'

'Because…because I'm not in danger now.' But she was. She really was.

He moved toward her slowly, a look of pure menace on his handsome face. 'Pretend you are.'

She shook her head. 'I can't.'

Eleanore didn't realise she was walking backward until she felt the cool press of the wall behind her. Lukas didn't stop until he'd placed his hands against the wall either side of her head. 'What are you going to do now, *moya krasavitsa*?'

Eleanore knew the word *moya* was the feminine version of *my* but as to the other word… 'What is it that you call me?' she asked huskily.

'What do I get if I tell you?' His own voice was low. Rough.

Me! the devil on her shoulder yelled, holding its hand straight in the air like an overzealous schoolchild trying to do the right thing, and boy, didn't she know what that felt like in her family! 'What if I promise not to hurt you if you do?' she said breathlessly.

He laughed. 'You couldn't hurt me if you tried.'

Goaded, she hooked her foot behind his calf, twisted and punched him in the stomach at the same time.

Her hand felt like she'd just smashed it into a warm brick wall and her only saving grace was that she'd brought him to the floor. Unfortunately he'd brought her along with him and she was now straddling his waist on the carpet, something her old instructor would not be pleased with. Still, she felt gleeful in her success and, slightly out of breath she threw Lukas a victorious grin. 'See. I got you down.'

'Did you?' His smile told her that she had only toppled him because he'd let it happen and then he smoothed his hands along the tops her thighs and all Eleanore could think about was the hard packed abdomen she was seated on top of. 'You should have let go of your bag as soon as that kid grabbed you,' he said gruffly, a strange expression on his face.

'I was holding on to the kitten,' she said dizzily, 'and anyway, I didn't realise what he was after. I would have given him money if he'd asked for it.'

Lukas shook his head. He didn't doubt that she would and emotion once again welled up from deep inside his chest.

He thought of all the times he'd tried a similar trick when he'd been about ten and how many people had walked past without even caring about some stray animal in need. All the kids in his sector had agreed it was an amateur's trick because if adults didn't give a damn about their kids why would they care about an animal? But Eleanore cared and the raft of emotions swelling inside of him threatened to break free.

The problem, he decided, was that she was like no woman he had ever come across before and he had no way of knowing how to handle her. Well, he knew one way, but a deep self-preservation instinct warned him that he shouldn't touch her.

'I've never met anyone quite like you,' he admitted absently.

She moistened her lips with the tip of her tongue and shifted her weight on his abdomen and every muscle in his body pulled tight. 'I'm nothing special.'

The words seemed to be wrenched from her throat and he knew she believed them.

'You're incredible,' he countered. 'Talented. Kind. Beautiful.'

'No.' She shook her head. 'My sisters—*oof*!'

She let out a squeak as he easily flipped her onto her back, holding most of his weight on his hands as he loomed over her. 'Your sisters would only be incredible because they share your genes.'

'Oh…' She gazed up at him, her eyes enormous in her lovely face, her lips soft. 'No one has ever said anything like that to me before.'

Something in her face, an innocent wonder he hadn't been expecting, gave him pause.

A distant memory of searching for his mother snuck into his brain as lethally as smoke from a burning building. Of those times he'd seen a woman with a similar stance to her, or similar hair colour, or with a tinkling laugh, and of him rushing up to her with adrenaline pumping through his young veins only to be hit by the devastation of having the woman turn around and be a complete stranger. It had been on one of those occasions that a woman had grabbed a nearby *politseyskiy* and he'd experienced his first beating at the hands of the law. Then he'd been sent to the state orphanage.

The orphanage he'd been on the verge of telling this woman about when she'd guessed his heritage before. Along with the fear and the beatings and the abject loneliness.

Der'mo.

Chemistry.

That was what this was. Nuclear strength admittedly, but chemistry all the same, and he was letting it addle his thinking. The fact was she was here to build his ice hotel and then she'd be gone. Sleeping with her would be nice—great, even—but ultimately a mistake and he was man enough to admit it.

So why did he still have her spread out on the floor beneath him?

As if guessing at his internal agitation she shifted, her thighs, and all those thoughts flew out of his head. She was smart and warm and good and so gloriously feminine. Everything a man could ever want. And he wanted her. Badly.

Slowly he lowered his body until his weight just rested over the top of her, his eyes fixed on her face.

Her eyes darkened with the same need

that was firing his blood, her cheeks pinking prettily.

'Lukas, I…'

'Talk too much?' He pressed his groin to hers and she made one of those soft feminine noises and bit into her bottom lip.

Unable to think any more, Lukas lowered his head and took her mouth in a searing kiss. No preliminaries, no finesse, just open-mouthed and hot. His tongue stroking over hers.

He felt her surrender in the soft whimpers she made and the way her arms curled around his neck, pulling him down to her. Lukas settled even more of his weight on top of her and registered her satisfied sigh. Registered the way her thighs widened to accommodate his bulk.

He pressed into her, control a lost cause. 'Eleanore,' he breathed, unable to think of anything but her.

Eleanore heard herself moan and tried to stop the desperate, needy sound in its tracks but it was impossible. She wanted to feel his mouth firm and hard on her body every time he looked at her and she was heedless to stop the desire that ran through her and burned her hotter than a ceramic kiln.

Lukas was making sounds of his own, deep, guttural sounds, and they made her feel boneless with desire. They made her feel like she was the most beautiful, the most desirable, woman on earth.

Ignoring all the reasons this was not a good idea her brain closed down and gave in to Lukas's rough lust that felt like exactly what she wanted. Exactly what she *needed*.

'*Bozhe*, Eleanore, you taste so sweet.' His mouth ate at hers and his hands impatiently caressed over her back, urging her closer, and Eleanore couldn't stop herself from pressing her aching breasts against his chest. He groaned and she wondered if he could feel the scrape of her hard nipples as pleasurably as she could feel the solid impact of his pectoral muscles.

With her mouth still consumed by his, Eleanore was only dimly aware that he had moved her sweatshirt up her chest. She had put on her best underwear—an antique lace–style set—after her shower and had nearly convinced herself that it wasn't because she wanted this to happen.

He paused and one finger traced the upper swells of her breasts. 'I take back what I said before. You're not beautiful. You're breathtaking.'

Uncaring of how desperate she seemed Eleanore writhed beneath him and pushed her lower body against his erection. 'Touch me, Lukas. Please.'

Lukas thought he might explode at her responsiveness and they weren't even naked yet.

Driven by primal lust he manoeuvred her sweatshirt up over her head and tossed it aside. He looked down at all her creamy skin, the delicate collarbones, the full breasts with their hard crests pushing against the lace of her bra.

Almost reverently he leaned down and stroked his tongue over those tight peaks through the lace and drew her into his mouth. Within seconds it wasn't enough and he grabbed the lace and yanked it down, groaning his pleasure as he sucked and licked her naked breasts.

This time she practically screamed his name and gripped his hair, massaging his scalp as he worshipped her body.

When her hips started circling upward he knew she was close, and dammit, so was he.

O Bozhe, but he was on fire for her.

'We need to take this to a bed,' he growled. 'But first I have to tell Ivan I don't need him any more tonight.'

'Ivan?'

Lukas rose to his feet and lifted her into his arms, striding down the hallway. '*Da*, my driver.'

He laid her on the bed and Eleanore felt the chill of the bedspread beneath her. Lukas reached into his back pocket and pulled his phone out and started punching the keys, his breathing laboured.

'No, wait!'

Sitting up she grabbed a pillow behind her and covered herself. 'You can't send Ivan home. He'll know.'

He glanced at her impatiently. 'He'll know what?'

'What we're doing?'

Lukas stilled and the hairs on the back of his neck stood on end. 'And?'

'And then everyone will know that we...that we...'

'That we?' He raised an eyebrow. Anger was replacing lust at a rapid pace and he wasn't about to make this easy for her.

She glared at him. 'Everyone will know that we slept together.' She said it as if they'd planned to rob a bank and she'd just realised how wrong it was.

'Last time I heard, it wasn't a crime for two consenting adults to have sex,' he said softly.

'No.' She wet her lips. 'But I work with you and...' She tilted her chin up. 'And I'm not willing to risk my job over this.'

Lukas couldn't believe she was serious. 'You think I'd sack you because we had sex?'

'Not this job. Harrington's.'

He frowned, his befuddled mind struggling to keep up with her thinking. 'Why would your job at Harrington's be at risk?'

'Maybe not at risk—at least I hope not—but everyone would assume that you hired me because I was sleeping with you.'

'Who cares what other people think?'

'I do,' she said stiffly. 'Your reputation might not mean much to you but mine means a lot to me.'

'Well, far be it from me to ruin your reputation *printsessa*,' Lukas scathed, irrationally angry that she was putting work ahead of him. Irrationally angry that he would put nothing ahead of her right now and didn't that just show him that he hadn't learned the hard lessons from his childhood as well as he'd thought he had.

As soon as Lukas stormed from the room Eleanore realised he had taken her comment the wrong way.

Grabbing a T-shirt from her drawer she quickly shoved it on and saw Lukas pacing around the living room in search of his jacket that was right in front of him on the back of a dining chair. 'I didn't mean it like it sounded.

It's just that if rumours started up about us and Isabelle heard...'

When she hesitated Lukas easily filled in the blanks. 'Your sister wouldn't offer you your precious promotion.'

She made a rueful face. 'Let's just say sleeping with you isn't going to win it.'

Logically he told himself that her attitude wasn't personal, that it was about her more than him, but as far as he was concerned logic could go to hell. 'Maybe she hasn't given you the promotion because you're not ready,' he sneered.

'I am so ready.' Her slender shoulders stiffened righteously and he immediately regretted the need to deflect his irritation onto her. 'I have a double degree and years of business experience. I started working at Harrington's during my summers when I was fifteen. I know the hotel industry inside out.'

'Are you trying to convince me or yourself? Because from where I stand neither one of us can give you what you want.'

'God, you can be hateful.'

He took in her flushed cheeks and her sparkling eyes. Saw once more that youth attacking her, felt again that knot of fear he hadn't felt for so long and never for someone else, and knew he had to get out of her apartment before he showed her that hate wasn't the only emotion he could make her feel.

'I'll organise the car to pick you up in the morning.'

'I can walk,' she said stiffly.

'After what happened tonight you'll take the car and if I hear you've ignored my instructions while I'm in London it won't be your job at Harrington's you'll have to worry about.'

Her chin lifted toward him. 'Is that a threat?'

'Yes, it's a threat. One you'd be wise to heed.'

She looked like she wanted to argue. She looked like she wanted to rip him a new one but instead she marshalled all those polite manners she'd been born with and kept her eyes steady. 'Have a good trip.'

Before tonight Lukas had intended to put off visiting his UK offices until after the ice hotel was completed. Now he decided it was the best thing he could do if for no other reason than to regain some of that iron-clad self-control his business rivals complained about. And maybe he'd rid himself of some of his pent-up sexual frustration with a woman who would appreciate it. 'Oh, I intend to,' he said before he turned and strode out of her apartment.

CHAPTER NINE

ONLY LONDON WASN'T the solace Lukas had hoped it would be. It was grey and tedious. So was Germany and so was Switzerland. And so were the women he had contacted and subsequently turned down.

He drummed his fingers on the walnut conference table and listened to his Swiss team talk about some of the exciting projects they were planning for the following year.

He should have been giving them his full attention but his mind wouldn't focus. Instead it kept drifting to a conversation he'd had with Petra an hour ago.

'The hotel is finished and everything is in place for the big party tomorrow night. The crew are all going out to celebrate tonight.'

He flicked a discreet glance at his watch. Were they already celebrating? It was still early but they'd just pulled off an impossible build that had taken long hours, including weekends, so he knew they'd have a lot of steam to let off. 'I hope you told them everything is on the house,' he'd told Petra.

'That's very generous.'

He'd heard the smile in her voice and grunted. Then he'd been unable to help himself. 'And Eleanore? Is she going?'

'Of course. The men all insisted. I think they've all grown really fond of her. She's a real trooper.'

Really fond of her...Lukas stewed on that. He knew she and Greg had worked closely together these past two weeks to finish the project. But how close? Were they even now clinking glasses and toasting each other. Smiling and getting a little tipsy. Tipsy enough to take their business relationship into the personal realm?

'Mr Kuznetskov? You look like you disapprove the idea?'

Lukas glanced up. '*Nyet, nyet*...I didn't say that.'

His finance manager smiled broadly. 'So it's a go? Frankly we wondered if we weren't pushing it a bit but the risk isn't *that* big.'

Knowing he couldn't tell the guy that he hadn't heard a word he'd said Lukas cleared his throat. 'Just, ah...just send the details through to my PA before you finalise things.'

'Right.' The man scrawled himself a note. 'Now the head of HR has some exciting…'

'Sorry,' Lukas said, rising to his feet and buttoning his single-breasted jacket. It was time he stopped kidding himself about where he wanted to be. 'I've just realised I need to get back to St Petersburg. I apologise for leaving early. Email me that exciting—' What had he said? *News? Plans?* '—information and I'll look at it over the weekend.'

Eleanore stared down at her shot glass of vodka. The men around her were chanting for her to down it and she rolled her eyes. 'One and one only,' she reiterated to the burly workmen around her with their beaming we've-just-finished-a-beast-of-a-job faces.

She crinkled her nose at the glass and tilted her head back. She had never been the shot glass kind of girl, not even at university, preferring beer or wine, but when in Russia… She held her breath and swallowed the clear liquid in one go.

Her co-workers cheered and someone clapped her on the back when she started coughing. Her throat burned and reminded her of the last time she'd accidently downed tequila a month ago at Glaciers. Then she'd been about to visit Lukas in his hotel room.

And why was she thinking of him again? She hadn't seen him for two weeks. Two weeks of peace where she and Greg had been left alone to complete the hotel. It had been bliss.

Of course she had kept Lukas apprised of what was going on. Short, professional emails that had matched the equally short and cordial tone of his.

Just the way it should have been between them all along. And thank God she'd come to her senses when she had. If she hadn't…if she hadn't… She didn't let her mind wander any further down that track. It was pointless. Career and men went together as well as lip gloss and windy weather and right now she was completely focused on the former.

Though there had been one good thing to come out of that night because Lukas's comments had prompted her to write a lengthy email to Isabelle outlining how she felt and what she wanted. She'd never done that before. At least not with Isabelle, but that was because she admired her so much and hadn't wanted to bother her. She never had done.

Back when they were kids Eleanore had been the pesky younger sister begging Isabelle to play dolls, or build Lego cities. Unfortunately Isabelle had been more interested in talking business with their father—even then—so Eleanore had often played alone or with Olivia when she'd had time. It had established a hero worship style of relationship between her and Isabelle that was probably well past its sell-by date.

And so far the only response she'd received to her email was that Isabelle would talk to her about it when she got to St Petersburg. Eleanore hoped the succinct reply had been because Isabelle was busy and not because she had pushed too hard.

'Another Stoli, Eleanore?'

Eleanore turned toward big Dominic and raised her hand in the universal sign of stop. 'Absolutely...' The word *not* stalled in her throat as she saw Lukas wind his way between all the raucous bar crowd toward them. He was casually dressed, like everyone else, in low-slung jeans and boots, a black sweater and matching puffer jacket and he looked long and lean and lethally attractive.

Lethally male.

All Eleanore's feminine hormones spiked at the sight of him and she told herself to forget about it. Told herself to forget how he kissed and how he tasted and how he smelt. Told herself to remember her goals.

'Why not!' she said, the insane devil on her

shoulder popping up at just the wrong time to take over her decision making.

Someone slapped her good naturedly on the shoulder and a glass was placed in her hand. Before she could bring it to her lips Lukas reached them and a cheer went up as everyone greeted the top. Over the weeks Eleanore had seen the admiration the men held for Lukas and it wasn't just because he was a generous boss. They respected his fairness and easy authority when it came to solving issues.

Contemplating the glass in her hand instead of the man in front of her, Eleanore blinked with surprise when Lukas reached out and removed it. 'One coughing fit is probably enough for one night. Don't you think?'

He smiled and Eleanore ignored the lift in her heart at the sight. So he was still the best-looking man she had ever seen. What did that mean anyway? It meant... She had no idea what it meant other than the fact that she had missed him. Missed him teasing her and challenging her and kissing her. Missed his sharp intellect. Not that she'd tell him that. No, she would be professional and polite because if there had been no point in encouraging the attraction between them two weeks ago there was even less when she was due to leave in two days' time. 'You took my drink.'

'You didn't really want it.'

'How would you know that?'

His mouth quirked at the corner. 'You crinkled your nose when you looked at it.' Eleanore's eyebrow rose and the quirk turned into a smile. 'You do that when you're not happy with something.'

'I do?'

'*Da*, listen.' He seemed slightly flustered and Eleanore couldn't remember seeing him like that before. 'Do you want a beer, a wine instead?'

Eleanore shook her head. 'Nothing. I...*we* weren't expecting you back until tomorrow.'

He leant his arm casually on the bar, as if he had nothing he'd rather be doing than talking to her. 'Change of plans. I wanted to congratulate everyone tonight since most of the men won't be around tomorrow.'

'Oh, right.' Of course his being at the bar had nothing to do with her, she knew that. And why would she even think that it had? 'How was London and Germany and Sweden?' she asked brightly.

'Switzerland.'

'Right. Switzerland.'

'Boring.'

'Oh.'

'How was it here?'

'Great.' It occurred to her that she was trying too hard to appear normal but she kept the cheery smile on her face regardless.

'I haven't stopped at the hotel yet but…you pulled it off. Well done.'

Eleanore felt a puff of pride inflate her chest. 'I told you I would.'

'Yes, you did.'

Her smile relaxed into a genuine curve and Lukas felt a possessive tug inside his chest. He should never have walked away from her that night. Why had he? It seemed a lifetime ago and he couldn't remember what had put him off. Certainly not her, she was the most beautiful woman he'd ever seen. And really there was only one thing to do about the chemistry between them and walking away from it wasn't the answer. She flicked her gaze from his to encompass the room and he wondered if the hunger that had him strung tight was too intense for her. He took a deep breath and pulled himself back when all he wanted to do was grab her by the hand and drag her somewhere private. 'So, have you decided when you're heading back to New York?'

She nodded. 'Sunday night. Isabelle is due to fly in tomorrow for the opening night party and then I thought I'd show her around the following day before we leave.'

'Any news of your promotion?'

Oh, God, this was torture, Eleanore thought. She hadn't expected him to show up like this and she couldn't seem to get her balance. She felt like a rat scrambling on a wheel thingy, running full pelt but getting nowhere. And her heart…it wouldn't stop beating a mile a minute. She felt so strung out she was getting a headache. How was it even possible to be so aware of one man in a room full of many? And what had he just asked her about? Oh, her promotion.

'Isabelle said she was going to talk to me tomorrow night. I'm quietly confident.'

'I'm sure once she sees the hotel she'll be impressed.'

'That's the general idea.' It had also been the general idea at Glaciers, she thought, only now realising how tense she was that her sister might not show up tomorrow night. 'Well…' She let out an exaggerated sigh. 'I think I'll call it a night.'

'Have you eaten?'

'No but…'

'Come to dinner with me?'

'Why?'

'Because I'm hungry and so are you and because I hate to eat alone.'

'You could ask any number of people at the bar to dinner and they'd go with you.'

He paused and Eleanore's heart thumped heavily inside her chest. 'I don't want to go with any number of people. I want to go with you.'

The look he gave her made it impossible to say no.

Because it was late Lukas took her to a hole-in-the-wall supper club that was discreet and unpretentious but stocked vintage champagne for those who knew about it. Lukas just happened to be one of those clients and he raised his glass in a toast. 'To a successful venture.'

Eleanore clinked her glass with his. 'I can't believe it's actually over. A couple of times I didn't think we were going to make it.'

She'd seemed to relax her guard with him over the course of the meal and opened up about her life in New York and her volunteer work at her local animal shelter.

He smiled as he recalled how at one point he'd thought she would bore him witless. Nothing could be further from the truth.

'What are you smiling at?' she asked, a little self-consciously.

Lukas had never been accused of being a foolish man and he wasn't about to prove the pundits wrong by admitting the truth now. 'The three-tiered ice chandelier?' he said, recalling one of the brief updates she had sent him via email.

'Please don't mention the chandelier.' She groaned. 'It fell twice during construction and Mikhail only just finished it this morning. I hope it's still hanging there tomorrow for opening night.'

'It will be. As will the horse-drawn sleighs and husky sleds out the back. Or did you think you'd managed to slip those past me?'

Her quick grin told him that that was exactly what she'd thought. 'It's a good idea. Everyone thinks so.'

'Everyone thinks the sun shines out of you. They wouldn't dare say anything else.'

She tried to pull off an innocent look but it only made him want to laugh. 'Are you upset?'

His eyes lowered to half-mast. 'Do I look upset?'

Eleanore's pulse sped up. 'Sometimes it's hard to tell with you.'

'I'm not upset. Have you been on one yet?'

She shook her head. 'I haven't had the time.'

'Maybe you'll have to visit our fair city again sometime.'

'I'd like that. It would be great to visit in the summer when the sun rises at four in the morning and sets at midnight. I can only imagine that everyone is completely exhausted the whole time.'

'You get used to it but heavy blackout curtains help.'

She laughed. 'New York is a little more civilised. The sun doesn't wake us until about six in summer.'

'You seem eager to get home.'

She hesitated, unsure how she felt about going home. 'I guess I am. It's been a while since I was there and it will be nice to see the city again. To spend time with my sisters.'

'You sound close?'

'Yes...'

'But?'

Eleanore thought about what he'd said about her sisters being talented because they shared her genes. She felt herself blush under his weighty gaze and forced her mind to concentrate. 'But we don't see one another nearly enough. No matter what though, they mean the world to me. What about you? I remember you said your parents are no longer here, but do you have siblings? Brothers or sisters?'

This was why Lukas never usually probed the women he dated for personal information. They usually probed right back. 'None that I know of.'

'Oh.' She tilted her head and her shiny ponytail slipped over one shoulder. 'That doesn't sound good.'

Lukas took a swig of his champagne and found his usual reticence to talk about these things strangely absent. What would she think if she knew the truth of his heritage? Would she be put off as he knew many other society heiresses would be? 'I didn't know my parents.'

'Not at all?'

'I was a street kid, Eleanore.'

'You lied to me.' She stared at him wide-eyed. 'When I asked you, you said…' She frowned as if she was trying to remember what he'd said.

'I think what I said was that you had a good imagination. And you do.'

She crinkled her nose but she didn't look away. Nor did she look disgusted. 'I'm sorry. That must have been really hard,' she said quietly.

Again his usual reticence to talk about his past deserted him. 'It was. It was also cold. And scary.' The words were out of his mouth before Lukas had time to check them and it made him a little uneasy. Not even Tomaso knew the intricate details of his early life. No one did.

'Can I ask what happened to your parents?'

It was the softness of her tone and the unwavering compassion behind her gaze that undid him. 'My mother left me on a train to Moscow.'

'Oh, that's terrible. She must have been heartbroken.'

It took Lukas a minute to realise that of course she would think it hadn't been deliberate and he nearly laughed. 'It was deliberate, Eleanore. She meant to—how do you say?—*ditch* me.'

'But…' Her brow furrowed as if such a concept was completely alien to her and perhaps it was. He was fast learning that far from being a shallow heiress she was a woman who felt things deeply. Which gave him pause although he couldn't figure out why.

'But…why?'

He realised he would have to finish the story even though he didn't want to he gave her the brutal honesty of his early life. 'My mother was a washed-up, drugged-out beauty queen and presumably my father was one of her many lovers. By the time I was five I was a liability she didn't want. We were living in squalor anyway so finding myself on the street wasn't that much of a stretch.'

'Except you were alone on the streets!'

Yes, he'd been alone. He'd been alone for a long time now.

'Before you morph into some kind of agony aunt,' he drawled, 'let me remind you that I am one of the wealthiest men in Russia. My mother did me a favour when she discarded me.'

Shock was etched into her wide hazel eyes. 'But how did you survive?'

'Like many of the thousands of other kids out there. You rob, you steal, you scrounge around in trash cans and sleep in train stations and drains. I was put into an orphanage at one point.' But that had been even worse. Full of people who looked at him with a mixture of pity and wariness. He'd lasted only a few months until he'd hit the streets again in search of his mother. Like Eleanore, something inside of him had still believed back then that it had all been a terrible mistake. That his mother hadn't meant to leave him alone and starving. He'd found out the truth soon enough.

'My life wasn't pretty but when I was sixteen Tomaso convinced his brother to give me a ride on his container ship. I didn't know much back then in the way of books and schooling but I knew enough to recognise an opportunity when I saw it and the rest, as they say, is history.'

'Survival of the fittest,' she murmured, repeating his earlier words. 'But what about the police? Couldn't you go to them?'

His soft laugh was full of scorn. 'The police aren't too fond of street kids, Eleanore. They sometimes hit the hardest of all.'

God, her childhood had been a fairy tale compared to his, Eleanore thought. Yes, she'd felt ignored at times and often not as good as her sisters, but she'd always known she was loved. Deep down. And yes, things had changed after her mother had died; her father had become remote and married another woman but he hadn't deserted her. He hadn't packed her off on a train to fend for herself.

'That's why you're building a school,' she murmured half to herself, remembering a conversation she'd had with Petra earlier in the week.

She'd come across a brochure for the St Petersburg Street Kids Foundation with a lot of photos of Lukas posing with a bunch of kids. At the time she'd thought it was promotional jargon playing to his vanity. A sort of *look at me—aren't I a great guy?* type thing.

Petra, of course, had waxed lyrical about how Lukas volunteered one morning a week when he was in St Petersburg and how he was currently trying to find a location to start a school that the kids could freely come and go from without recrimination. Somewhere they would feel safe, she had said.

Naturally she had assumed that Petra had exaggerated to make Lukas sound like a prince. Now she wondered if in fact he wasn't one.

'What do you know about it?' he asked gruffly.

'Only what Petra mentioned.'

'That woman has been with me for far too long.'

'So it's true?'

'Kids are usually on the streets because they have nowhere to go. Or at least nowhere safe.' He shrugged. 'I have the means and the resources to help and the inside knowledge on how they think. It was a logical decision.'

Logical my foot, she thought. He cared. He *really* cared.

She gazed across the table at him. She felt terrible that she had pushed him to tell her about his childhood, pushed him to dredge up those dark times, and she just wanted to go to him and wrap her arms around him and tell him that if she'd known him back then she would have found a way to take care of him. A way to keep him safe.

As if reading her mind he scraped back his

chair and stood up. Eleanore gazed up at him, very afraid that the evening was over.

'Enough with the morbid details of my life.' Lukas saw the pity in Eleanore's eyes and didn't like it. It was way past time he stopped talking about things he'd all but forgotten about. He reached out his hand for her. 'I want a tour of the Krystal Palace.'

'Now?'

'Why not?'

'Well, it's empty, for one.'

Lukas smiled. 'Hopefully the last time it will be with any luck, and the perfect time to go through it. Wouldn't you say?'

Eleanore didn't know what to say. She only knew that she didn't want the night to end just yet.

CHAPTER TEN

THE HOTEL LOOKED majestic as they approached. The large construction fence had been removed and the ice building glowed with a mystical energy set off by well-placed blue, pink and golden lights that phased in one after the other.

When they pulled up in Lukas's black Ferrari two warmly dressed security guards greeted them but other than that the hotel was silent in the freezing night air as they went through the double glass doors and into the empty foyer.

Eleanore snuggled deeper into her overcoat and pulled her *ushanka* down over her ears. Lukas smiled and placed his hand in the small of her back.

Everything was softly lit and the ice sculptures of unicorns and snow wolves and nymphs that Eleanore had commissioned stared down at them as they passed.

'So maybe not quite alone,' she murmured.

Lukas chuckled and glanced at the domed roof. 'There's your glass-topped ceiling.'

'Yes. And that wasn't easy. It's held up by reinforced steel inserts at the top. I'd like to take all the credit for its construction but really it was your engineer who worked out how to keep it safely in place.'

Lukas gave her a look. 'I think you're too modest, Miss Harrington.'

Eleanore shrugged. 'Anything like this is a team effort.'

He didn't say any more but followed her through the maze of corridors that led to the various rooms.

Still having the master keycard Eleanore was able to access all of the guest suites.

Lukas made all the right noises when he spotted the tropical fish tank over the top of the ice futon and Eleanore could tell that he particularly liked the Bedouin tent set in a desert oasis with a heated outdoor spa that was completely private. He was equally impressed with the fifteenth-century Louis XV boudoir and the Australian bush shack but his eyes took on a particular light when they reached the captain's cabin of an old pirate ship.

Stepping back, Eleanore let him go in ahead of her.

This was still her favourite room with its

large porthole-shaped windows, antique desk carved from ice with a treasure map etched into the top, the admiral's chair covered with lamb's wool and the large ice globe of the world that could be spun. The pièce de résistance though was the elaborately carved four-poster ice bed with real red velvet drapes that dominated the room. Lukas walked over to it. 'Sturdy.'

Eleanore held her breath. There was no missing the expression on his face and it took her breath away.

'Do you imagine being tied to it?' he asked her softly.

'No!' Yes. Maybe… Her heartbeat picked up and heat raced through her blood instead of oxygen. She didn't think she was a prude but tied up? She hadn't even had sex yet!

Her pulse beat fast beneath her skin. They were all alone in the hotel. Just the two of them, and a deep sense of inevitability swept over her. She wanted this man. She had wanted him even before she had met him and it seemed that he wanted her too.

'You don't sound convinced,' he said softly.

Eleanore stared at him. Would it be so bad to give in to the desire coursing through her? Her career was on track—she hoped—and it wasn't as if one night with a man was going to derail her long-range plans. And anyway, who made the rule that she couldn't temporarily deviate from her goals now and then? Just because she hadn't before didn't mean it would be catastrophic, did it?

'I've told security I'll be staying here tonight.' His deep voice brought her back to herself. Back to him.

'You did?'

He came toward her. 'I believe an hotelier should always try out his hotel to make sure it's up to standard.'

Eleanore couldn't take her eyes from his. 'That's very forward thinking of you.'

'I'm a very forward-thinking kind of guy.' He stopped directly in front of her and Eleanore could feel the heat coming off him. Absently she wondered how the ice sculptures around them were still standing.

'For instance.' He took hold of her gloved hands and pulled her slowly closer. 'I've already imagined you without the overcoat and that soft-as-butter sweater beneath. Without those figure-hugging jeans.'

Eleanore stared up at him. He was seducing her. And, oh, she wanted him to…she wanted… 'Lukas…'

'I missed you.'

She'd missed him too, but she was scared.

He made her feel so much. Too much, maybe. She'd tried to forget about him these past two weeks. When that hadn't worked she'd tried to hate him. But she didn't hate him. She didn't know what she felt but she knew she might never have another chance to be with a man who fired her blood the way he did and if she didn't seize this moment she might be left wondering what she had missed. And wasn't that a tragic thought?

She shivered.

'Are you cold?'

She shook her head. She wasn't cold. She was hot. Burning hot.

Seizing the moment Eleanore reached up and wound her arms around his neck, fitting her body to his. Lukas groaned and tore his thick gloves off with his teeth. They fell unseen to the floor, along with her *ushanka*, and then his warm fingers were in her hair and his mouth was on hers and, oh, it felt so right.

Eleanore kneaded the strong muscles in his neck and pulled him in close. The kiss went on and on before he wrenched his mouth from hers.

'Tell me you want me,' he said, his hands unbuttoning her overcoat before running over her torso and back, moulding her closer.

'Is this some ego thing?' she asked, her

hands slipping beneath his puffer jacket to stroke his lean waist. She moaned as his mouth skimmed down the side of her neck and bit down gently on her flesh.

'*Da*. Most definitely.'

'I want you,' she said as he pushed her coat to the floor and followed it with her jumper. She shivered, both at the cold air on her skin and the heated gaze from Lukas's blue eyes. He lifted his hands and traced along the edge of her simple bra before palming her breasts in his big hands and strumming over her nipples with his thumbs. 'Oh, I want you.'

And she did. Desperately, all thoughts of pulling back from the fire she was afraid might consume her driven out by searing lust and overriding passion.

Desperately she clutched at his shoulders and would have fallen if he hadn't pushed his thigh higher between her legs and cupped her bottom to hold her against him. She whimpered this time and forked her fingers through his thick hair. 'I *really* want you.'

His chuckle was husky and sexy and before she knew it he had scooped her up and carried her to the big bed. 'We're going to have to do this under covers or you're going to catch a chill.'

He whisked back the luxurious crimson

fleece blankets and laid her on the soft fleecy layers below that were designed to be sealed together like a cocoon. Right now though she didn't want a blanket on top of her, she wanted Lukas, and she reached up and pulled him down to her.

'Soft,' he murmured as he captured her lips again.

'All the beds are designed for comfort,' she said.

'Not the bed.' He leaned up on one hand and tugged her bra cups downward before reaching around to release the catch to get rid of it altogether. His lips lowered and he blew a warm breath over her chilled flesh. 'You.'

He drew one of her tight nipples into his warm mouth and Eleanore arched up off the bed. Thinking became almost impossible but she knew she wanted to see him this time.

Her hands went under his sweater and met firm, hard skin and he went still as she explored the thick layer of muscle that covered his back. Then she brought them forward to his wide chest and his big body shuddered above her.

Eleanore felt a wicked thrill that she could affect him so much and trailed her fingers along the downy hair that bisected his abs.

Lukas swore and reefed his sweater off over

his head. Eleanore gazed up at him avidly. If possible he was even more beautiful with the mat of dark blond hair covering his lean muscles.

'Lukas…' She didn't know what she would have said but he distracted her when he flicked open the buttons on her trousers and yanked them down her legs.

He took a second to admire her silky underwear and then they were gone as well.

Eleanore didn't have any time to feel embarrassed because he came over her again and brought his mouth first to hers and then to her breasts and then lower.

She couldn't do anything else but grip his shoulders as he nuzzled and kissed his way around her belly button. Every one of her senses was attuned to where he was going and then finally she felt his light kisses on the outside of her thighs before he moved inwards.

Stunned by the petite beauty of her body Lukas moved his hand between her thighs. 'Open your legs for me, Eleanore. I want to see you.'

An almost shy expression crossed her face and he had a moment of remembering how he had watched her sleep that first night and thought her so innocent. Like now as she gazed up at him in wonder as if no man had ever touched her like this before. And deep inside it disturbed him to realise that he wanted that to be the case.

'Lukas…'

Realising he had become caught up on thoughts he'd never had before, he placed his hand on the flat of her belly and moved it lower. 'Is this what you want, *moya* Eleanore? Do you want me to touch you here?'

He curved his hand over the neat centre of her femininity and just revelled in the shape and feel of her.

'Yes, oh, yes. I want…I want…'

Lukas didn't wait for her to finish telling him what she wanted because he wanted it too and he lowered his head and teased her with the tip of his tongue.

She gripped his hair and Lukas succumbed to the taste and feel of her. Never before had he nearly come from going down on a woman but he was about to now and he lathed her with his tongue one last time before climbing back up her body.

She was whimpering and going crazy beneath him and Lukas quickly lost his trousers and donned a condom with shaky hands. Then he resettled himself in the cradle of her thighs and nudged at the entrance of her body. This…

this was heaven and nirvana and paradise and everything a man could ever ask for in life.

'Eleanore…' He didn't know what he'd been about to say but as her silky wetness covered him and prepared him for her body he gave into the force of a need he'd never felt before and drove smoothly into her warm centre.

She stiffened instantly and so did he when he realised that her body was fighting the invasion of his rather than welcoming it. 'Eleanore.'

'I…' Clearly stunned she stared up at him with unfocused eyes.

'Eleanore, please tell me you've done this before,' he begged hoarsely, knowing that she hadn't.

'I… Oh, Lukas.' She wrapped her arms around his back and groaned softly as she tried to pull him in tighter.

'Don't move, *moya lyubov'.*' He cupped his hands either side of her face and eased his bulk off her just a fraction. 'Let your body adjust.'

'It's okay. It doesn't hurt now.'

Now!

In a state of amazement that Eleanore had never taken a lover before Lukas didn't know whether to continue or to pull out. He knew what he wanted to do but this wasn't just about him. To say that he was shocked was an understatement. 'Do you want me to stop?'

She shook her head and he reached down and released her ponytail. She shook her hair out and her lower body gripped him hard.

Lukas bit back a groan and nearly spilled himself inside her there and then.

'Pull your legs up around my waist,' he instructed roughly.

She did, her eyes watching him as he started to move in and out of her body with long smooth strokes. 'Tell me if I hurt you,' he said, gritting his teeth.

She sighed his name and he felt her tight sheath relax enough to take him all the way into her body. Slick with perspiration and unable to control himself any longer Lukas gave into the animal inside of him and moved more powerfully inside her, watching her face the whole time for any sign that she wanted him to stop.

Fortunately that didn't happen and when her orgasm gripped hold of her Lukas did something he'd never done with any other woman as his body joined hers in an exquisite release that went beyond the realm of normal: he looked into her eyes and kissed her.

The first time Lukas woke it was to find Eleanore snuggled into his side, her head on his shoulder and one leg draped over his, both of them buried beneath thick fleecy blankets that kept out the icy coldness of the room.

There was just enough early-morning light being filtered in through the ice bricks that Lukas could make out her sweet profile and see the warm puffs of her breaths as they met cooler air.

Lukas lay on his back and stared at the red velvet drapes cocooning them in a secret world. He gently pulled the fleecy blankets more firmly over Eleanore's shoulder and tried to figure out how he felt.

His head seemed to be full of emotions he wasn't used to feeling and he couldn't decide if he should get up and leave or hold her tighter.

He pressed his nose to her hair and inhaled apples. A smile formed on his lips. He'd never eat an apple again without thinking of her. His hands drifted to her hair and he gently twirled a strand around his finger. He didn't want to wake her. She looked so peaceful. So beautiful. So innocent.

Or not so innocent any more.

He frowned. She'd been a virgin. The realisation still shocked him. He never would have expected it and yet he should have because the sense of pureness about her was one of the first things he'd noticed. He released a shaky breath. Had he hurt her? He manoeuvred his stiff shoulder out from under her head just a little so he could look down at her.

She sighed and shifted closer, curling her hand into the hair on his chest.

Giving in to an urge he couldn't quite understand he bent forward and kissed her. Softly. Not enough to disturb her but…she lifted her chin when he drew back as if even in her sleep she couldn't help seeking him out. He smiled again.

'Lukas…' Her voice was a sleepy whisper of silk in the quiet room.

'I'm here.' His was more like a rumble. He cleared it. Pressed his lips to her again in a feather-light kiss.

'Mmm, that was nice.'

She still hadn't opened her eyes and Lukas bent to her again and kissed her sweetly. He didn't need to have sex with her. He was content just to touch her but then she arched into him like a cat and before he knew it he had rolled her onto her back and was poised over the top of her.

'Are you sore, *moya krasavitsa*?'

'No.'

The second time he woke it was panic stations.

'Oh, Lukas, Lucky!'

Dressed in her jeans and sweater she hopped

around on one foot as she pulled her boot on. Lukas's gut tightened with a sense of urgency to right whatever was wrong. He frowned. 'What's lucky?'

'The kitten. I forgot to feed him last night. He'll be starving.'

Lukas collapsed back against the pillows. 'Relax. I'm sure he's gone a lot longer without food.'

'He's not going hungry on my watch.' She stood over him and gazed at him as if in some acknowledgement that he himself had gone without food at one time and a lump formed in his throat.

An emotion that seemed to create more pain in his chest than pleasure gripped him and he eased out a quick breath.

Briefly he thought about pulling her back down to him and then she mentioned something about getting a cab if he was too busy. Yes, he was too busy. Too busy imagining her naked. But she wasn't taking a cab and he told her so as he rolled out of bed and yanked his jeans on.

She was quiet during the drive to her apartment and he wondered if she was regretting the night before. Or perhaps she was regretting being seen by the hotel staff they'd had to pass on their way to his car. His jaw clenched.

It shouldn't bother him that she relegated work above him; after all, he'd been guilty of doing the same thing with women his whole life, but for some reason it did.

Probably because right now he had the craziest thoughts torpedoing through his brain and a knot in his belly. Crazy thoughts of Eleanore in his apartment. Eleanore in his bed. Eleanore in his *life*. But she was leaving. Tomorrow, in fact.

She was busy checking her messages while he drove and suddenly a smile as big as the sun lit up her face. 'She's coming. She's really coming! Isabelle's coming!'

Lukas frowned. That kind of dependency was dangerous and he wanted to protect her from it. 'You know you don't need your family to succeed, Eleanore. You're extremely talented and capable in your own right.'

'I know that.'

Her response was clipped and he was sorry he'd interfered. And why had he? It wasn't as if she was his responsibility, or that she had asked for his opinion.

Brooding on that he decided to drop her at the kerbside outside her apartment and go clean up at his. But when he turned into her street there was a parking spot right outside the building. So okay, he'd walk her to her door. But then he'd leave.

Only he didn't leave. He followed her inside. Saw the filthy kitten that was no longer filthy but looked as if it had visited a pet day spa. The animal nuzzled her and she nuzzled it back and he felt a moment's jealousy. Of a cat!

'I should go.'

'Oh, sorry. We both need to take showers and start the day. Let me feed Lucky and I'll see you out.'

He waited, feeling antsy.

She walked toward him with a shy smile on her lips that made her so damn cute. 'So, uh...'

Lukas grabbed her and pulled her into him. 'You mentioned a shower.'

The third time he woke up he was alone. It took him longer to orient himself this time because he was coming out of a sex-induced coma that seemed to suck him down deeper every time he and Eleanore made love. When he realised he'd fallen into a deep sleep in her bed he scowled.

He thought about the conversation they'd had from the hallway to the bathroom.

'Why didn't you tell me you were a virgin?'

She'd stiffened in his arms and he'd cursed his bluntness.

'Does it matter?'

It did but he wasn't sure how. Other than to give him some caveman sense of pride in being the first man to touch her so intimately. The first man to give her such pleasure. The first man to join his body with hers. Not that he would be the only man to do those things, he reminded himself. When she returned to New York she'd have plenty of men after her... plenty of lovers who would kiss her and stroke her smooth skin. Plenty who would watch her as she climaxed. Lukas cleared the uncomfortable thoughts from his head.

Naturally enough he hadn't said any of that at the time. He'd told her that of course it didn't matter. Well, it did, he'd said, but only in the sense that if he'd known he would have gone slower. Been more gentle. And perhaps he might not even have started anything, though there was no guarantee of that.

'It was fine,' she'd said. And then she'd frowned up at him in the bright light of the small bathroom, her hair like a tousled brown cloud around her creamy shoulders. 'How was it for you?'

'Velikolepnyy,' he'd answered truthfully.

'What does that mean?'

'Magnificent.'

And it had been true. Touching Eleanore

seemed to go beyond the basic physical need for release he usually experienced with a woman. It seemed to reach into the very core of him and make him feel warm.

He, who hadn't noticed the cold in so very long.

Then she'd smiled that slow, sensual smile of a woman just coming into her own power and scattered his wits like a summer breeze.

'Yes, it was,' she had said, reaching up to stroke his stubbled jaw. 'And the other word? What is it that you call me?'

'Beauty.' He'd yanked her sweater over her head, cupped her breasts in the palms of his hands. '*My* beauty.'

A banging sound further down the hallway brought his mind back to the present. He heard a muffled curse and smiled. Probably something to do with the cat.

He thought about the last time he'd woken up in a woman's bed. It wasn't that uncommon an occurrence, though it had been a while. What was uncommon though was waking up with a woman in his arms.

Growing up pretty much alone meant that he was used to a lot of space. And he liked it. Now he found the empty bed beside him more disconcerting than welcome and that he wanted Eleanore back in his arms.

Clearly one night was not going to be enough to quench the fires still raging inside of him. Even now he was ready to go and that wasn't like him at all. But okay, it was nothing to panic about. He liked Eleanore. And he *really* liked having sex with her.

In fact, it was not only the best sex he'd ever had but it had been fun. What they'd done in the shower…the way she had used her mouth… He groaned. She was a fast learner and now he was hard again.

Time to get up.

A sweet smell greeted him as he rose from the bed. Was that…? He sniffed the air and stepped into his jeans. Was that baking? Surely a career woman like Eleanore wasn't baking.

He heard what sounded like the oven door slamming shut and pulled his sweater over his head. He walked into the kitchen and stopped dead.

Eleanore was dressed in a slinky silk robe with what looked to be nothing underneath; her feet were bare and her hair was put up haphazardly with those silly chopsticks she'd had in her hair the first time he'd met her. And yes, she most definitely had been baking if the hot pan full of something on the granite bench was anything to go by.

Lukas felt his blood chill.

Then something soft and alive brushed his ankles and he nearly jumped out of his skin.

Eleanore glanced up. She smiled when she saw him but the smile on her face dimmed just as quickly as it had appeared. 'What is it?'

'What's that?'

She gave a small laugh. 'Muffins. I thought you might be hungry.'

Muffins. Biscotti. An old need he'd had as a kid to belong rose up inside him and the knot in his belly returned. It was a need that terrified him. It whispered to him that his life wasn't as perfect as he liked to think it was. That there was more out there. But there wasn't. Not for him. He'd learned that the hard way.

'Lukas, what's wrong?'

'Nothing.' He cleared his throat. 'I just didn't realise you were a domestic goddess.'

'A domestic goddess?' She frowned. 'Why does that sound like an insult?'

'It's not.' His gaze shifted to the main door. 'I just thought you women's lib types would head to Starbucks instead of the kitchen.'

'I beg your pardon?'

'Look, I have to go.'

Eleanore stared at the man who had made love with her so completely the night before and again that morning to the point that she thought she'd expire from the bliss of it.

It was a feeling she'd thought he had shared but now he was looking at her as if he'd like nothing more than to erase the time they'd spent together from his memory banks.

Heat rose up in her face. It had all seemed so perfect. *He* had seemed so perfect. Last night he'd said he had missed her; he'd told her she was beautiful. And she'd felt so happy that she'd gotten up and baked muffins.

Somewhere between deciding to go to bed with him and this moment she'd forgotten that last night was just a temporary hiatus for both of them.

'Tell me,' she said with a coolness she was far from feeling, 'have you ever made a woman a cup of hot chocolate after sex?'

His brows shot up his forehead. 'Hot chocolate?'

'That's what I thought.' And if that didn't stop her from wanting more from him then she didn't know what would. 'Well, goodbye, then. Have a great…day.' Life. Whatever.

Irrational emotions bloomed inside her chest and Eleanore turned away and headed toward the bank of windows in the living area. She suddenly felt lonely. Really lonely, just as she had after her mother had died.

'*Bozhe*, Eleanore.' He swung her toward him and hauled her into his arms before she could take a breath. Eleanore resisted. She really did. But his mouth was so hot and hungry on hers and she just ignited, her body moulding itself to his without permission from her brain.

'I'm sorry, Eleanore. I don't know what just happened. Sometimes I'm *glupo*. This is one of those times.'

'I don't know what *glupo* means.'

'Stupid.'

'No, I shouldn't have expected you to stay for breakfast.'

He kissed her again and Eleanore felt her determination to resist him crumble under the warm pressure of his skilful mouth. God, the man could kiss.

'Yes, you should, but I do have to go,' he murmured. 'There's a lot to do before opening night tonight.'

'I know.' Part of her had been hoping that maybe they could spend the day together given that she was flying home the next day but she wasn't going to come across all desperate. Not when she'd woken up and thought how easy it would be to fall in love with a man like him. A man who was capable and strong and tender and so easy to talk to. Those kinds of thoughts didn't fit into her game plan. And they obviously didn't fit into his either. 'I have a lot of things to do myself,' she said. 'But I'll see you later on at the party, right?'

'Right.'

Eleanore stood statue still as he closed the apartment door. Then she went back to the bench and picked up a muffin. Broke a piece off. Her orange notebook lay on the small table by the window and she brushed the crumbs from her fingers and picked it up. Flipped it to the last entry. She read her current goals.

Flipped back through her others. Every year she spent part of her New Year's Day reassessing. Her current list hadn't changed for three years. Before that her degree had dominated the number-one spot.

She'd been writing down her goals ever since her mother had died. Ever since she'd arrived home from primary school and raced down to her mother's bedroom to give her a clay bird she'd painstakingly modelled in class only to find the room empty. Sometime during the day her mother had passed away and no one had told her. Of course they'd meant to and her family made a great fuss of her afterward but the desolation of finding her mother's bed empty and remade as if she'd never existed had never left Eleanore.

She had felt like a little rowboat that had accidently come away from its moorings and was drifting out to sea. So she'd made a secret scrapbook about her mother and hidden it in her wardrobe and brought it out when she'd been at her lowest. Writing down the things she needed to achieve in a journal after that had been a natural progression. Reading over them had helped to ground her. Helped her to keep things real in her head. But had she become a little bit obsessive about those goals? A little bit rigid?

'I must say I'm surprised to see marriage way down on your list.' Lukas's comment from weeks ago came back to her. He'd said it only made her more attractive to him. She went over the scene they'd just had in her kitchen. Fortunately, he wasn't the type who would ask her to reprioritise her goals so why was she even questioning them?

Lukas paused behind the wheel of his car after leaving Eleanore's apartment. What had just happened up there? One minute he'd been thinking about inviting her to spend the day with him and taking her to a couple of buildings he was thinking of purchasing for his school and the next he'd panicked. It had been those damned cookies. Or muffins or whatever the hell they were. No woman had ever baked for him other than Maria and she was sixty.

She baked for anyone and everyone. When he'd found Eleanore in the kitchen looking like, yes, a domestic goddess, he'd felt special.

He released a shaky laugh and realised that his hands were trembling. He tightened his grip on the steering wheel. For all he knew Eleanore baked all the time as well and passed her wares around like confetti. She'd told him earlier on that she could cook so… He chuckled and let out a long breath.

Special?

What a fool.

Clearly the sex had fried his brain cells. That was all that had just happened.

CHAPTER ELEVEN

'ELEANORE, YOU'VE DONE an amazing job.'

Eleanore beamed at Isabelle and gave her a quick hug. 'I'm just so happy you came.'

'I apologise for missing the opening of Glaciers. Work has been crazy busy.'

'That's okay. It's water under the bridge. How's Olivia?'

'Getting married.'

'I just heard! And to a Chatsfield... I can't wait to meet him.'

Isabelle tossed her dark hair behind her shoulder. 'Please don't mention that name to me. Of course I'm happy for Olivia but going to family Christmases will be untenable if Spencer happens to be there. Those ones I might have to miss.'

'He still giving you grief?'

'He gives me nothing but grief.' Something sparked in her sister's eyes but Eleanore couldn't place it. Was it pain? Had Spencer done something to harm her?

'Issy, are you okay?'

'Fine. I'd rather not talk about Spencer though. I'd rather talk about your email.'

'Oh, right. I was a bit fired up the day I wrote it but…'

'Don't apologise. I thought it was excellent. And you're right. You should have more responsibilities within Harrington's.'

'Really?' Eleanore blinked, wide-eyed.

'Really.' She paused and Eleanore could almost hear a drum roll. 'How does Vice President of Business Development Australasia sound?'

Eleanore nearly dropped her mocktail. 'Come again?'

Isabelle smiled. 'I'm really sorry, El. I've been so caught up in getting the business up to speed since Dad died I should have thought of it earlier.'

'Vice president…' Eleanore grinned. 'Are you kidding me?'

'You don't want it?' Isabelle teased, smoothing her hair behind her ear.

'Of course I want it but…'

Isabelle's dark brows drew together. 'But what?'

Yes, Eleanore, but what?

'But…' Eleanore tried to work out the mixed emotions tumbling around inside her stomach.

This was everything she had dreamed about and more and yet even now her eyes were seeking out Lukas. She hadn't seen him since they had parted ways that morning and she'd been hoping to walk in with him to gage his reaction to the gala opening. Watch him turn those bright blue eyes on her as he took in the bar staff and their swanky, specially lined black tie jackets, the waiters on ice skates carrying silver trays filled with canapés above their heads, and the who's who quaffing special drinks designed by Lulu for the night.

But he hadn't been there and no one had seen him. A chill went down her spine at the thought that he might not show up. He would. Of course he would.

'Eleanore?' Isabelle prompted.

She shook off her weird feelings and injected enthusiasm into her voice. 'Will I have to move to Australia or something?'

'Not necessarily but you might have to base yourself over there. I was thinking Singapore. Australasia encompasses a wide area and you'll need to spend a fair bit of time there. We can work out the finer details later.'

'Of course.'

'You are happy, aren't you, El?'

Eleanore smiled. 'Of course. I'm just...overwhelmed.' And she'd like to talk to Lukas about it. Share her news.

'Tell me, how bad was it working for Lukas Kuznetskov?'

'Not bad at all as it turns out. He's different than we first thought.'

Isabelle pulled a face. 'I find that hard to believe. His reputation as a hard-nosed businessman precedes him.'

'As yours precedes you,' she teased her sister.

Isabelle tossed her a rueful look. 'I hope so. I have a feeling I'm going to need it.'

The heaviness behind her sister's words was impossible to miss and once again Eleanore noticed her brown eyes cloud over. 'Okay, Isabelle, what's up?'

Isabelle sighed. 'It's just Spencer. I think he's planning a takeover bid and I'm worried I won't have the votes.'

'How many do you have?'

'Since Olivia sold me her shares I've got thirty-five and a half per cent. Not enough.'

'Maybe I should sell you mine. That would give you forty-nine per cent.'

'I can't take your shares.'

'Why not?'

'They're your legacy from Dad.'

Eleanore shrugged. 'It's not like I need them.

And if you give me the same rate as Olivia, then I'll be happy.'

'Seriously, Eleanore, decisions like that aren't made on the spot. You at least need to think it through.'

Eleanore smiled as she recalled telling Lukas the same thing once. Of course he hadn't listened. 'Okay, I'll think about it. But just know that you have my vote no matter what. You've done an amazing job at Harrington's and there's nobody else more qualified to run it.'

But interestingly enough while she didn't need to think about selling her shares if it gave Isabelle more of a sense of security, Eleanore wasn't exactly feeling like dancing on the spot at Isabelle's offer of a promotion.

She scanned the room again and spotted Lukas at the top of the grand staircase on the mezzanine level. He was wearing a tuxedo and he was heart-stoppingly gorgeous. Relief flooded her system and she must have made a faint noise because Isabelle followed her gaze.

'Lukas Kuznetskov?'

Eleanore couldn't take her eyes off him. 'Yes.' Her heart took off in her chest and the rest of the room faded out as their eyes connected. She felt Isabelle go still beside her.

'Is there something you're not telling me, Eleanore?' Isabelle had on the mothering tone she'd perfected even before their mother had died.

'No.'

But her voice was a squeak and Isabelle's dark brows climbed her forehead. 'You've always been a terrible liar.'

'Oh, Issy, I slept with him.'

The words tumbled out of her mouth before she could stop them and it was such a relief to say them.

Isabelle gaped at her, completely silent. Finally she let out a small cough. 'When?'

When Lukas's attention was snagged by someone beside him Eleanore forced her gaze back to her sister's. 'Not before I completed the job, I assure you.'

Isabelle frowned even more. 'I don't care about the job. I'm just shocked. You've never done anything like that before and he's so... so...'

'Gorgeous? I know.' Eleanore sighed. 'I can't quite believe it myself.'

'Oh, El, you're in love with him. Please tell me I don't have another sister about to walk down the aisle?'

Oh, how she wished.

What? Sorry?

Eleanore dragged in a rushed breath. Where had that come from? She wasn't in love with Lukas and she certainly didn't want to marry him. She wanted to take up the role of VP of Business Development Australasia. *Didn't she?*

Before she could regain her composure the man himself stood before them.

'You must be Isabelle Harrington.'

Lukas held out his hand and Isabelle automatically took it. 'I am.'

'I'm Lukas Kuznetskov.'

'Yes, I know.'

Oh, please, Issy, don't say anything about marriage! She knew Lukas would run a mile if she did and her sister was wrong. Completely wrong. She wasn't in love with him.

'Eleanore was just telling me all about you.'

Eleanore struggled for breath and refocused on what Isabelle was saying.

'Was she?'

'The hotel,' she rushed out, 'I was telling her about the hotel. About building the hotel. About how well it went.' Eleanore didn't know who she was trying to protect by steering the conversation toward work, but she babbled on about the build and the complications until she was short of breath.

To her mind Lukas grew more and more distant with every word she said. Exactly as he had been that morning. He cleared his throat politely. 'As you can see, your sister is a marvel and well in need of a promotion.'

Isabelle smiled. 'Is that right?'

'*Da*. It is. Now if you'll both excuse me,' Lukas said. 'I'll leave you to talk.'

He moved away and Eleanore felt bereft.

'Well, well, well,' Isabelle said. 'That was interesting.'

Eleanore didn't think it was interesting at all. She felt sick. Something was up with Lukas. Either that or it was her. 'Issy, I just need to talk to him. Can you give me a minute?'

'You sound upset.'

The last thing Eleanore wanted was Isabelle's protective streak rising to the fore.

'No, I'm…I just…I'll be back.'

'Take your time. I've just spotted the owner of Westlake's and want to sound him out on a business idea.'

Eleanore gave her a faint smile and went after Lukas.

She stopped him just before he got to the ice bar. 'Hi. When did you get here?'

'About an hour ago.'

An hour ago! And he hadn't come to find her? 'Oh.' Something was definitely wrong.

'Did you get your promotion?'

Why was his voice so cool?

She frowned. 'Yes. VP of Business Development Australasia.'

Lukas whistled. 'Congratulations. That's impressive.'

'Thanks.' It was impressive but Eleanore was suddenly struck by the knowledge that she wanted to ask him for his opinion. She wanted to ask him what she should do. Lukas would no doubt laugh at her if he could hear her thoughts. They were so far from a feminist's perspective she'd be excommunicated if she were a member. 'It's all still sinking in,' she said.

'You'll take it, no doubt.'

She eased out a slow breath. He didn't want her any more. That was becoming clear at an astonishing rate. Perhaps he had even found someone else to spend the night with. Someone he was even now going to meet. 'Of course I'll take it. I'd be a fool not to.'

Da, Lukas thought, *of course she would take it*.

She was a woman who knew how to prioritise and she never let her heart rule her decision making. He should have been grateful. Sex was sex and she wasn't going to complicate what they'd shared with any messy emotional outbursts or demands. He had to respect that.

Only what they had shared hadn't felt like just sex to him and that was one more reason he needed to put some distance between them. His life was perfect the way it was. The problem was he was still thinking with the wrong head.

He looked down at her, so cool in her slim-fitting trousers and emerald-green sweater that brought out the green shards in her eyes. The orange boots and for once no orange chopsticks to match. Really, she wasn't clinging and she wasn't crying. He should be rejoicing. He was getting exactly what he wanted. A woman who put work ahead of relationships.

The perfect woman to match his perfect life.

'A happy ending all round,' he said.

'Yes,' she agreed woodenly. It felt strange to talk to him like this when all she could think about was being in his arms.

'Are you still flying out with your sister tomorrow?'

Eleanore nodded.

Lukas nodded as well.

Ask me to stay with you tonight, she thought. *Tell me last night was special for you.*

'That's good.' He stepped back from her just

when she thought he was about to pull her into his arms. 'I'm flying out too. To London.'

'When?' She hid her disappointment with a big smile.

'In a few minutes.'

In a few minutes!

Eleanore smoothed her hands down her thighs. 'You just got back.' A sick feeling started to spread out from the pit of her stomach like the venomous tentacles of a blue-ringed octopus, smothering what was left of her happy mood.

'Business never stops, you know that.' He dug his hands into his pockets. 'But I'll try and fly to New York next weekend,' he said briskly. 'Will you be there?'

'Yes. At least I think so.' Eleanore felt dazed but kept up the facade of having it all together. 'I haven't worked out all the details of the job offer with Isabelle yet.'

Lukas nodded. 'Then I'll call you first.' He turned away, took a step and then turned back. His hand reached out and stroked down the side of her face and Eleanore's toes curled inside her boots.

Tell him how much last night meant to you. Tell him you can't wait to see him again.

Her chin came up. 'See you.'

When he walked away without a backward

glance she knew two things. One, Isabelle was right and she had indeed fallen hopelessly in love with him, and two, he had no intention of calling her.

CHAPTER TWELVE

ONLY SHE WAS WRONG. He did call. He called to
say he couldn't make it.

Eleanore sipped her white wine from a long-
stemmed glass and automatically moved on to
view the next painting of an up-and-coming
New York artist as someone made space in
front of it.

When he'd called he'd asked about her job.
Asked how she was. Even asked about Lucky.
Then he'd promised to see her the following
weekend but he'd had to cancel that as well.
Not that he'd called this time. He'd just sent
an apologetic email. Which was why she was
filling in for Isabelle at a corporate event by
herself. She'd been hoping he would fly in and
they'd put in an appearance together and then
go back to her place. Which made her feel foolish because, really, she was just extending the
inevitable which was that he would eventually
move on and she would return to her original

goals. Of which number two—an investment property—had just moved up to the number-one spot.

Unfortunately the very idea of hunting for any type of property right now made her want to throw herself under her covers and stay there till next year. Somehow after she'd left Russia her goals had lost most of their urgency.

She knew what it was, of course. It was Lukas and coming to terms with the fact that she had finally fallen in love and it was with a man who had pursued her right up until the moment she stopped being a challenge. Not that he'd made any secret of that, or any promises to the contrary. No, this sense of misery that seemed to follow her around like her own personal rain cloud was her own fault.

She'd known what he was like; heck, she'd warned Lulu away from him... And... A thought pierced her as true as an arrow shot from an Olympian's bow. If he had asked her to stay the night of the gala opening she would have jumped at the chance. A silly hormonal impulse that would have stood her well for all of maybe two weeks before he had grown tired of her and moved on, leaving her not only heartbroken but jobless as well.

No, this was better. Much better.

A wrenching sob nearly broke free from her

throat and Eleanore pressed the heel of her hand against her breastbone to stem the pain.

She'd told Lulu that men and careers didn't mix. This was just more evidence of that. So okay, she'd had one sensational night with him and it had meant so much more to her than it had to him. She would get over it eventually because what choice did she have?

'Eleanore Harrington?'

Eleanore turned to find a well-dressed New York executive beside her. He was just a fraction taller than her and stocky, like a boxer, but he carried himself like a man born to wealth. A banker perhaps. Or a property tycoon. They were thick on the ground at gallery openings. 'Yes.'

He offered her his hand to shake. 'My name is Peter Bournesmith from Bournesmith Real Estate and I'm very pleased to run into you.'

Eleanore shook his hand. So not quite a property tycoon, but close. 'Why is that?' she asked, feigning interest. She had to be interested in something, didn't she?

'I visited the Krystal Palace last week and I was very impressed with the scale and vision of the project.'

She noticed that he had blue eyes. Not as bright as Lukas's. More a deep-ocean colour. But dull and... She pulled her thoughts up and gave herself a mental rap across the knuckles. Took a deep breath. 'Thank you but it wasn't all my doing. A fair bit of the plans for the hotel were in place before I came on board.'

'Nevertheless I am in the process of building a group of elite condos in Dubai for a very wealthy client of mine and I could use a woman with your attention to detail and architectural capabilities.'

Was he offering her a job? It was almost funny, only she wasn't in the mood to laugh.

'I'm sorry,' she said, 'but I only consulted on the Krystal Palace as a one-off. I work for Harrington's.'

'Ah.' His eyes studied her. 'Have you ever considered going into business for yourself?'

Lukas's words from over a month ago suddenly jumped into her head.

Staying in a company for family reasons can limit your true potential.

But it wasn't her family limiting her true potential, was it? It was her. She'd been wedded to her goals for so long because they gave her an element of control over her life. An element of certainty that had made her feel safe.

But they hadn't saved her from heartbreak and maybe it was time to open herself up to some other possibilities. Maybe it was time to start believing in her abilities instead of waiting for her family to do it for her. Maybe it was time to explore the world outside of Harrington's. But could she really leave Harrington's at a time when Isabelle seemed to need her the most?

'I can see I've got you thinking,' Peter Bournesmith said.

Eleanore shook her head. 'Not really.'

But even she heard the quaver in her voice and being a true salesman Bournesmith went in for the kill. He handed her his business card. 'How about I buy you a drink and we can talk about it some more. Maybe we could hit a club afterwards.'

While the thought of returning to her flat on a Friday night wasn't all that appealing neither was the idea of making small talk with a man she wasn't interested in. And really there was no competition when Lucky, a bucket of ice cream and the latest movies online were waiting for her. 'Thanks, but no thanks,' she said, sidestepping the event photographer on her way out.

'I miss Eleanore.'

Lukas looked up and scowled at Petra as she dumped a load of mail on his desk. He grunted at her and kept his attention on the sales projections for a new company he was thinking of investing in.

'Have you heard from her?'

Lukas rubbed his jaw. 'Why would I hear from her?'

'I thought she might have called to find out how the hotel is doing? It's been two weeks already.'

'If she wants to know how it's going she can call the hotel directly or read the reviews on-line like everyone else.'

'Mmm.' She fossicked around his desk. 'I suppose she's busy back in New York. She certainly looks busy.'

Since he was trying to zone Petra out it took a minute for her words to penetrate his mental blocks. 'What do you mean she looks busy?'

'I just saw her photo online at an art gallery talking to some nice young man. Is there anything else I can get for you?'

'No.'

His eyes narrowed on her figure as she bustled around watering the plants in the corner of his office. He told himself that he was not going to do a Google search on Eleanore and art galleries. But it seemed his fingers had other ideas because he'd typed the words on his keyboard before he could stop himself.

He'd spent the past couple of weeks forgetting about Eleanore Harrington and the month she had been in his life. Two weeks forgetting about the taste of her skin and the sound of her laughter. Forgetting about the smart mouth she was never afraid to use on him when he stepped out of line. And forgetting about the incredible smile she was directing toward the suit in the photo on his computer screen.

He scanned the caption underneath. Eleanore Harrington and Property Developer Peter Bournesmith Cosy Up at Top Gallery.

Cosy up?

Well, she certainly hadn't wasted any time getting busy with someone else. While he'd been putting in twenty-hour days at his desk she'd been out partying. But what had he expected? That she'd miss him? That she'd *pine* for him?

'You could go after her.'

Lukas realised he'd been staring at the image on his screen and turned away from it. 'Why would I want to do that?'

'Because you fell in love with her.'

Lukas shook his head. 'Sometimes I don't know where you get your ideas.'

'Maybe it was the way you used to look at her.'

Lukas gave Petra a look and it wasn't the I-love-you variety.

'And from the fact that you've been like a bear with a sore head ever since she left.'

'I did not look at Eleanore a certain way and

I've been busy.' He turned back to his computer to emphasise the point.

'You're always busy but you're never difficult to work for. I remember telling Eleanore that I loved working for you. Right now I want to quit.'

Lukas blinked at his PA. 'You can't quit.'

'And I'm not the only one.' She continued on as if he hadn't even spoken. 'You've been barking at the staff for two weeks. Nothing is good enough for you.'

'Maybe my standards have been raised.'

'I certainly hope so. I've never approved of the other women you've dated.'

'I wasn't talking about my personal life and I did not date Eleanore Harrington.'

'Then maybe you should,' she huffed. 'Anything is better than living in this space.'

Lukas surveyed his luxurious office. 'You have a problem with my office?'

'I meant your mental space.' Her voice softened. 'It's not healthy, Lukas. I worry for you.'

'You're not my mother, Petra. You're my PA.'

She sniffed. 'I'm sorry I care.' When she turned and stalked from the room Lukas searched his desk for something to throw.

Der'mo.

He glanced up at the image of Eleanore smiling on his screen. Had he fallen in love with her?

It didn't seem possible but every single muscle in his body bunched at the thought and his heart kicked painfully behind his breastbone.

There was no denying she had somehow profoundly changed him. The usual solace he found in his work had been missing ever since she'd come into his life and lately he'd even found himself unintentionally preparing his own list of goals in his head. Always in those unconscious moments the number-one position was family and number two was Eleanore.

Usually at that point he'd deliberately bring to mind the sick sense of desolation he'd felt when Eleanore had chosen her work over him which was usually when he replaced *that* emotion with anger. At himself.

He tapped his fingers rhythmically on his desk. The only other time he'd felt that depth of despair was when he'd been twelve years old and he'd found his mother on a normal city street. After that he'd vowed he'd never chase another woman again.

Was that what he was thinking of doing now? Chasing Eleanore? He pressed the heels of his palms against his eyes. His future yawned in front of him. A future without Eleanore in it. A heavy coldness seeped into his bones and he was once again that fearful little boy all alone on the train to Moscow.

Only he wasn't that boy any more. He was a man. A man who had choices. A man who had fallen in love with a beautiful woman who was too good for him. It was unexplainable and unwanted but there it was.

Love. He let the word roll around inside his head for a bit. Tapped his desk some more. He saw Eleanore with the kitten, the way her face softened with tenderness. He saw the way she looked when she climaxed. The way she had looked at him when he kissed her. He thought about how much she made him laugh.

He swore and shoved his chair back from his desk. He had no idea if she really wanted him in her life. He had no idea if she would reorder her list of goals for him but he knew he had to try.

He stopped beside Petra's desk. She didn't look up. 'I apologise.'

She sniffed again.

Lukas smiled. Clearly females with attitude were his specialty and he hadn't even realised it. 'Would it make you feel better if I ask you to organise the jet to fly me to New York?'

This time she looked up. 'Infinitely.'

Was five o'clock too early for wine?

Eleanore kicked off her high heels and sighed as her feet sank into the deep carpet.

Lucky wound his way between her legs. 'Hello, baby,' she crooned. 'Miss me?'

He purred and she picked him up. She discarded her suit jacket on the bed. Lucky rolled around on the duvet as she changed into old sweats and an even older Cornell sweater and finished the ensemble off with a pair of ratty old socks that were soft and warm. Then she carried Lucky into the kitchen and checked the circular wall clock that was designed to look like an old fob watch.

No, five o'clock was definitely not too early for wine.

'Not that you want wine, I know that.' She picked up the empty saucer of milk from the floor and refilled it with the special kitten milk from the pet shop.

While Lucky lapped it up she went to her fridge and poured herself a glass of Riesling she'd had in there for ages.

And anyway, it was a celebratory drink. Today she'd finalised the sale of her shares to Isabelle and told her that she wasn't going to take the VP job in Australasia. Her sister had been shocked but Eleanore had known it was the right decision as soon as she'd said it. Instead she'd informed Isabelle that she was going to use the money to start her own consulting and design firm.

Things would be slow at first, she knew that, but she was ready for the challenge and Isabelle had said that once she'd squashed the Chatsfields' attempted takeover bid she'd invite her to join the board so that she could still be a part of the Harrington brand. Eleanore smiled at the thought. It felt good to finally feel on equal footing with her sister.

So all in all it had been a great day.

And to make it a great night she'd eat her leftover brownies from the day before with the tub of ice cream she'd just picked up from Whole Foods. She also had a copy of her favourite romantic film on DVD to sit in front of.

A text message pinged on her phone and she pulled it out of her handbag. Her heart sped up just a little but it was only from the businessman she'd met at the gallery. Since she'd refused to have a drink with him he'd texted her a couple of times to invite her out for dinner. Both times his text had come in late in the afternoon and what sort of man invited a woman out at the last minute anyway? One who'd been stood up, she suspected.

It was almost as bad as a man telling you he'd call and then not doing so. Not that Lukas hadn't called. He had but he hadn't kept his promise to come and see her. And okay, maybe he hadn't promised but—dammit, she wasn't going to think about him again. It caused an ache in her chest not even Ben & Jerry's Boston Cream Pie could ease. The only thing for it was to go cold turkey and not think about him or talk to him again. Which was why she jumped whenever her phone rang. It was because she *wasn't* going to answer it if his name flashed up on her screen, not because she was.

When someone rang her doorbell she nearly jumped out of her skin again. Since her building had security it must be a neighbour. A desperate neighbour by the sound of how quickly they rang again. Probably it was Penelope's new boyfriend who had locked himself out again.

Smiling she opened the door mid-knock. 'Hello, Simo—' Her heart stopped. It wasn't her neighbour's boyfriend at all; it was Lukas dressed in a crumpled suit he looked like he'd slept in. He hadn't shaved either which wasn't usual for him. 'Lukas! What on earth are you doing here?'

'Who's Simon?' He scowled. 'He's not the guy in the picture?'

He pushed past her before she could take in the fact that he was even standing on her threshold and she swung around to follow him down her short hallway to her living room. 'What picture?' She held up her hand and noticed it was shaking so she stuck it on her hip instead. 'What are you doing here?'

'I told you I was coming to town.' He glanced around her small comfy living room.

'Actually, you told me you *weren't* coming to town.'

His gaze returned to hers and she had the oddest sense that he was nervous. He flashed his movie-star smile and she knew she'd been wrong.

'Nice place.'

'I don't care what you think of my place,' she said, fighting to keep her emotions at bay. 'I'd like you to leave.'

He ignored her and walked over to her low coffee table and picked up her glass of wine. 'Only one glass. Does that mean you're not expecting Simon?'

Simon?

Not waiting for an answer he sniffed the plate of brownies. 'I know these are not biscotti.'

'No, they're brownies.' She moved closer and snatched the plate from his hands. 'What are you doing here?'

'You answer my question and I'll answer yours.'

'I can't remember your question.'

'Are you expecting Simon? Or perhaps that guy from the art gallery?'

Eleanore narrowed her eyes. 'Are you trying to insult me? Simon is my neighbour's boyfriend. And how do you know about Peter anyway?'

'Petra saw the photo of the two of you together.'

'It made the news?'

'See?' He smiled faintly. 'I'm not the only one who doesn't read their own press.'

'I hardly think it's the same as…'

At that moment Lucky snuck his head out from beneath the sofa and wound himself around Lukas's legs. Half expecting Lukas to ignore him, Eleanore was surprised when he bent down and picked him up. He stroked his fur and the two of them stared at each other for a minute. Then Lucky lifted his nose to Lukas's for a cat kiss. Eleanore wanted to tell him not to waste his time. That his affections were fickle.

'He's grown.'

'Yes.' Her throat was clogged and her knees started trembling as it set in that Lukas was really standing in her living room. 'Lukas, please tell me what you want? Is it something to do with the ice hotel?'

'It's nothing to do with the hotel.' His gaze shifted from her to the view outside her windows and then straight back. 'It's you.'

'Me? What have I done?'

'You haven't done anything. Well, you have but…I want you.'

He saw the moment recognition of what he was saying lit her eyes and she wasn't happy.

'That's cheap. You couldn't find any other woman in Russia to have sex with?'

Lukas might have laughed if he didn't feel that his whole life was hanging in the balance. She was angry with him so that had to be a good sign. Anger was better than apathy. Or worse, pity. Wasn't it?

He took a deep breath. 'I don't want to have sex with any other woman in Russia. Or London. Or anywhere.'

'Too bad…'

'I want to make love with a woman in New York.'

'I hope you brought your little black book with you.'

'You, *moya krasavitsa*. I want to make love with you. For ever.'

She blinked at him as if she couldn't understand what he'd said. 'I beg your pardon?'

'Tell me that *popka* from the art gallery is not important to you.'

'That what?' She frowned. 'Never mind. Would you forget him? He's nobody.'

'Ah, that is music to my ears.'

Lukas stepped closer to her and threaded his fingers through hers. When she didn't immediately pull away his heart beat a little quicker. He breathed in deep and the scent of apples calmed him.

'Lukas, I...'

'I've missed you. I've missed looking at you and talking to you. I've missed touching you and just holding you. I know I don't deserve you but I want you, Eleanore. No one else can drive out the coldness inside me the way you can.'

Eleanore felt dazed. 'I don't understand.'

'It is simple. I love you.'

'If that were true...if it was, then why did you cancel the past two weekends?'

His hands squeezed hers. 'Because I was terrified. Right from the start I knew you were different from any woman I had met before and I didn't dare let myself hope for more. Then when I saw how happy you were over your sister's job offer at the party I expected you to choose Harrington's over me and you did.'

'But you didn't let on that you wanted anything else from me. Not seriously.'

'I know my actions don't seem to make sense but...after my mother abandoned me I tried to find her. For years I searched for her without success. And then one day I did. I stumbled across her in the street. I was sure I was mistaken. She was with a man. I don't remember him, but I do remember her. To me she was the most beautiful creature I had ever seen and I can't explain the joy I felt in that moment; the sense that finally I wouldn't be scared any more. That I wouldn't be alone.'

Eleanore's heart gripped at the pain she saw etched onto Lukas's face. 'What happened?'

Her voice seemed to rouse him from a nasty place no child should ever have to go and he glanced at their joined hands as if he only just realised he was holding her. He smiled faintly. 'She pretended she didn't know who I was.'

'Oh, Lukas.'

'Then she walked away and she took my heart with her. After that I vowed I would never feel that vulnerable again. I vowed that I would never risk feeling anything for a woman again. I can't seem to help it with you.' His eyes held hers. 'I love you, Eleanore. I love everything about you.'

Eleanore felt a watery grin slip across her face. 'You do?'

'Completely. Totally. *Absolyutno.*'

Tears trembled on her lashes. She loosened his grip on her fingers and reached up to wrap her arms around his neck, burying her nose against his chest. 'I love you too. I love you so much it scares me.'

Lukas kissed her. An endless kiss that drove any lingering doubts about how he felt right out of her head.

'I can't believe it.' She stared up at him. 'I thought…I thought that you were just playing a game with me. That once I'd capitulated you didn't want me any more.'

'Not want you? Eleanore, *moya lyubov*, it is not humanly possible to want you more than I do. You make me feel whole. You make me feel warm again. I've been so miserable these past two weeks Petra has threatened to quit.'

'Petra? I don't believe it. She adores you.'

'And fortunately she's canny enough to know that I adore you. That my life is empty without you in it.' He took her face between his hands. 'I've thought about this a lot and I want the whole package, Eleanore. Marriage. Kids.' Lucky wove between their legs, purring. 'A cat.'

'Oh, Lukas. I want that too.'

'And I know your goals are important to you and that your new positon in Australasia is…'

'I'm not working for Harrington's any more,' she interrupted. 'You helped me see that in many ways I was using Harrington's to prove my worth to my family—and myself—and that

I'm limiting my true potential by doing that. So I've skipped along to goal number three and decided to start my own consulting business.'

'Consulting?'

'I'm good at it.'

Lukas gathered her closer. 'You are.'

Her smile made his heart soar. 'Any idea where you want to set up this business?'

'I'm not sure. Maybe in *Rossiya*.'

Lukas winced at her botched pronunciation. 'Not until I've taught you a few Russian words perhaps.' He smiled but his tone turned serious. 'But really, Eleanore, if you want to stay in America, then I can shift my headquarters to here.'

'You would do that? You'd leave St Petersburg?'

Lukas turned her face up to his and kissed her sweetly on the lips. 'I would do anything for you. Don't you know that by now?'

She leaned into him. 'I would never ask you to leave because I know the school you want to build is important to you and the kids need you. But maybe we could divide our time between the two?'

'Whatever makes you happy, *moya krasavitsa*. Which reminds me.' He released his hold on her. 'I have something to show you.'

He dragged her to the window that overlooked her quiet street and raised the squeaky sash. Curious, Eleanore lent her head outside and a wide grin split her face. 'It's a horse-drawn carriage!'

'*Da*. I organised a sleigh from Boston but there is not enough snow in New York to drive it.' He gave her a lopsided grin. 'I am hoping this alternative is still considered romantic.'

She gazed at the ornate carriage and waved at the uniformed driver. 'It's *very* romantic.'

When she turned back inside Lukas was on bended knee with a ring box in his hand and a definite look of nervousness in his eyes. He cleared his throat. 'I was going to wait until we were in the carriage but…about goal number four?'

Eleanore's grin consumed her face as a feeling of happiness threatened to burst right out of her chest. 'What about it?' she whispered.

'I'm hoping to make it goal number one.' He opened the box and the most exquisite emerald ring sat nestled in a bed of red silk. 'Eleanore Harrington, I don't know what I have done to deserve you in my life but I promise to adore you and love you and take care of you for all of our days. If you'll have me?'

Tears slid down her cheeks unheeded and Lukas stood to wipe them away.

Eleanore raised trembling hands to his face

and gazed at the man who had stolen her heart. 'Yes, yes, I'll have you. Yes, I'll marry you.' She kissed him softly. 'How do you say "I love you" in Russian?'

'Ya tebya lyublyu.'

When she repeated the words back to him Lukas grinned and grabbed her around the waist, swinging her into a high embrace. 'Maybe you can just show me, *moya* Eleanore.' He slid his hands to her bottom and urged her legs up around his waist so she was under no illusion as to what he meant.

She smiled. '*Da*, maybe I can. Always.'

* * * * *

If you enjoyed this book, look out for the next instalment of
THE CHATSFIELD:
TYCOON'S DELICIOUS DEBT
by Susanna Carr
Coming next month.

LARGER-PRINT BOOKS!
GET 2 FREE LARGER-PRINT NOVELS PLUS
2 FREE GIFTS!

⊕ HARLEQUIN®

INTRIGUE
BREATHTAKING ROMANTIC SUSPENSE

HILP15

LARGER-PRINT BOOKS!
GET 2 FREE LARGER-PRINT NOVELS PLUS
2 FREE GIFTS!

♦HARLEQUIN®

Romance

From the Heart, For the Heart

YES! Please send me 2 FREE LARGER-PRINT Harlequin® Romance novels and my 2 FREE gifts (gifts are worth about $10). After receiving them, if I don't wish to receive any more books, I can return the shipping statement marked "cancel." If I don't cancel, I will receive 4 brand-new novels every month and be billed just $5.09 per book in the U.S. or $5.49 per book in Canada. That's a savings of at least 15% off the cover price! It's quite a bargain! Shipping and handling is just 50¢ per book in the U.S. and 75¢ per book in Canada.* I understand that accepting the 2 free books and gifts places me under no obligation to buy anything. I can always return a shipment and cancel at any time. Even if I never buy another book, the two free books and gifts are mine to keep forever.

119/319 HDN GHWC

Name _____ (PLEASE PRINT)

Address _____ Apt. #

City _____ State/Prov. _____ Zip/Postal Code

Signature (if under 18, a parent or guardian must sign)

Mail to the Reader Service:
IN U.S.A.: P.O. Box 1867, Buffalo, NY 14240-1867
IN CANADA: P.O. Box 609, Fort Erie, Ontario L2A 5X3
Want to try two free books from another line?
Call 1-800-873-8635 or visit www.ReaderService.com.

* Terms and prices subject to change without notice. Prices do not include applicable taxes. Sales tax applicable in N.Y. Canadian residents will be charged applicable taxes. Offer not valid in Quebec. This offer is limited to one order per household. Not valid for current subscribers to Harlequin Romance Larger-Print books. All orders subject to credit approval. Credit or debit balances in a customer's account(s) may be offset by any other outstanding balance owed by or to the customer. Please allow 4 to 6 weeks for delivery. Offer available while quantities last.

Your Privacy—The Reader Service is committed to protecting your privacy. Our Privacy Policy is available online at www.ReaderService.com or upon request from the Reader Service.

We make a portion of our mailing list available to reputable third parties that offer products we believe may interest you. If you prefer that we not exchange your name with third parties, or if you wish to clarify or modify your communication preferences, please visit us at www.ReaderService.com/consumerschoice or write to us at Reader Service Preference Service, P.O. Box 9062, Buffalo, NY 14240-9062. Include your complete name and address.

HRLP15

LARGER-PRINT BOOKS!
GET 2 FREE LARGER-PRINT NOVELS PLUS
2 FREE GIFTS!

HARLEQUIN

super romance

More Story...More Romance

YES! Please send me 2 FREE LARGER-PRINT Harlequin® Superromance® novels and my 2 FREE gifts (gifts are worth about $10). After receiving them, if I don't wish to receive any more books, I can return the shipping statement marked "cancel." If I don't cancel, I will receive 4 brand-new novels every month and be billed just $5.94 per book in the U.S. or $6.24 per book in Canada. That's a savings of at least 12% off the cover price! It's quite a bargain! Shipping and handling is just 50¢ per book in the U.S. or 75¢ per book in Canada.* I understand that accepting the 2 free books and gifts places me under no obligation to buy anything. I can always return a shipment and cancel at any time. Even if I never buy another book, the two free books and gifts are mine to keep forever.

132/332 HDN GHVC

Name	(PLEASE PRINT)	

Address		Apt. #

City	State/Prov.	Zip/Postal Code

Signature (if under 18, a parent or guardian must sign)

Mail to the **Reader Service:**
IN U.S.A.: P.O. Box 1867, Buffalo, NY 14240-1867
IN CANADA: P.O. Box 609, Fort Erie, Ontario L2A 5X3

Want to try two free books from another line?
Call 1-800-873-8635 today or visit www.ReaderService.com.

* Terms and prices subject to change without notice. Prices do not include applicable taxes. Sales tax applicable in N.Y. Canadian residents will be charged applicable taxes. Offer not valid in Quebec. This offer is limited to one order per household. Not valid for current subscribers to Harlequin Superromance Larger-Print books. All orders subject to credit approval. Credit or debit balances in a customer's account(s) may be offset by any other outstanding balance owed by or to the customer. Please allow 4 to 6 weeks for delivery. Offer available while quantities last.

Your Privacy—The Reader Service is committed to protecting your privacy. Our Privacy Policy is available online at www.ReaderService.com or upon request from the Reader Service.

We make a portion of our mailing list available to reputable third parties that offer products we believe may interest you. If you prefer that we not exchange your name with third parties, or if you wish to clarify or modify your communication preferences, please visit us at www.ReaderService.com/consumerschoice or write to us at Reader Service Preference Service, P.O. Box 9062, Buffalo, NY 14240-9062. Include your complete name and address.

HSRLP15